THE SPIDER:
THE WITHERING DEATH

MASTER OF MEN !

THE WITHERING DEATH

By Grant Stockbridge

POPULAR PUBLICATIONS • 2022

PUBLISHING HISTORY

"The Withering Death" originally appeared in the December 1938 (Vol. 16, No. 3)
issue of *The Spider* magazine. Copyright 2022 by Argosy Communications, Inc.
All rights reserved.

CHAPTER 1
GRISLY RENDEZVOUS

"THERE IT is, Dick—rather an odd calling card, eh?" Wilbur Patterson grinned wryly as he shoved across the mahogany top of his desk a brownish hued, seared skinned relic that at first glance appeared to be the dried foot of a large bird.

At first glance—and then Richard Wentworth realized that he was looking at the mummified remains of a *human hand!* A man's left hand, the bony fingers hooked like talons, as if avidly clutching, even in death. Burned into the shrunken skin of the back was a message that fairly leaped out at him—*Disobedience means death!*

"When did you receive this thing, Wilbur?" Wentworth's keen, hard eyes lifted from the grisly relic to the puzzled, worried face of his friend.

"I found it here on my desk that afternoon." The wealthy inventor and explosives manufacturer shrugged. "An hour or so before I phoned you. It's the work of some lunatic probably," he laughed uncertainly. "He has been annoying me for the past week with hollow-voiced telephone calls demanding ridiculous sums of money—and this seems to be the follow-up."

He went on. "At first I was minded to throw the filthy thing out. Then I thought of you and retrieved it from the wastebasket for your benefit. You like to play around with myster-

1

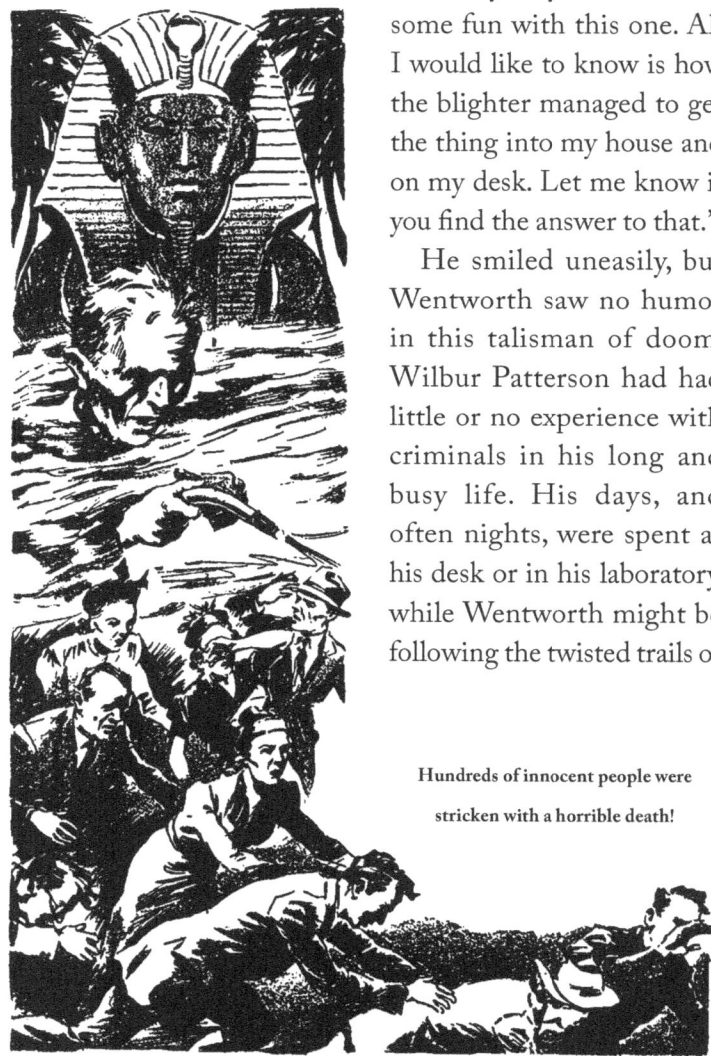

Hundreds of innocent people were
stricken with a horrible death!

ies. Maybe you can have some fun with this one. All I would like to know is how the blighter managed to get the thing into my house and on my desk. Let me know if you find the answer to that."

He smiled uneasily, but Wentworth saw no humor in this talisman of doom. Wilbur Patterson had had little or no experience with criminals in his long and busy life. His days, and often nights, were spent at his desk or in his laboratory, while Wentworth might be following the twisted trails of cunning thieves and murderers—the sort of scheming criminals whose warped brains might be instigating grisly horrors that to normal men would seem incredible.

Wentworth's jaws tightened. "I don't want to scare you, Wilbur," he said simply, as he wrapped the mummy hand in a handkerchief and dropped it into the pocket of his topcoat, "but I will ask you to be careful. Let me know promptly if you hear anything more from this fellow. Nita is giving a little dinner party, and I should be there now. However, I'll tackle this thing in the morning and see if I can find that answer for you."

He, realized that nothing was to be gained by alarming the old man unduly. Yet the picture of that shriveled hand, that seemed to be clutching from the grave, would not banish from his mind. Even when he had joined Nita van Sloan and her guests, the memory returned and worried him—so much so that she sensed it and a half-frown flitted over her face....

NITA KNEW that she was not envious, as her violet eyes flickered from pretty Evelyn Marlowe to handsome, distinguished-looking young Peter Hennessey, and then flashed across the perfectly appointed little dinner table to the strong-featured, vital face of Richard Wentworth. A thrill of pride tingled through her, glowing warmly around her heart as her glance met his and read the fond admiration in his keen, blue-gray eyes.

In the affection of Richard Wentworth, she possessed something that was infinitely precious, she told herself for the thousandth time. He was one man in millions—capable of holding any woman completely and filling her life to overflowing. Certainly Nita was not envious... and yet the open devotion of these two subtly whetted the longing that, it seemed, must always be a part of her own life.

Evelyn Marlowe had completed her musical training, made her debut abroad, had sung on the coast and in Chicago. Now her operatic career was to reach a triumphant climax in a series of New York concerts that Peter Hennessey was sponsoring. At the conclusion of the series she and the wealthy young socialite were to be married and leave on a round-the-world honeymoon. It would be only a matter of a few more weeks....

No, Nita envied Evelyn nothing of her happiness, but a half-sigh still rose involuntarily in her breast. She, too, had dreamed of a honeymoon abroad. Time and again she and Dick had made eager, exciting plans, and more than once they had had their preparations almost completed. But always she had known that, no matter what they might plan, the final decision would not rest in their own hands. It lay in that deep, inner urge which motivated Richard Wentworth's whole life.

Tonight, at this little dinner party in her Riverside Towers apartment, Dick was all that could be asked as a charming host and entertaining companion—yet beneath his smiling, ready conversation, she sensed that tenseness gripped him. Something was *wrong*, she felt convinced of this even though Dick had not uttered a single word to indicate it. Something was holding his attention, keeping his nerves taut, even while he concealed it perfectly from their unsuspecting guests.

Nita knew him far too well to be deceived. They had been through so much together, were in such complete rapport, that pretense between them was impossible. Tonight he had arrived promptly, had given no indication that anything was amiss—and yet the moment her telephone rang she realized that she had been waiting for its ring as tensely as he.

That call was for Dick. Even before Lola, her maid, came in to make the announcement, Nita was certain of it.

Wentworth's flat-planed, poker face was impassive as he rose and excused himself. But Nita did not miss the flicker of excitement in the shadowy depths of his deep-set eyes. In the lithe, pantherish stride with which he left the room, she read the ready answer to any challenge that might come. Instantly, the phone's ring had seemed to transform the affable, companionable Richard Wentworth his friends knew into the grim, bleak crimefighter men called the Spider. At this very minute, the call to danger might be sounding in his ears—the challenge that he could never resist....

IT WAS Jackson, his chauffeur and right-hand man, who was on the wire when Richard Wentworth picked up the receiver. "Perhaps I should not disturb you, sir," Jackson apologized, "but a Mr. Kenneth Rockwell has been trying to reach you. He called twice, and this time he seems so anxious that I said you would phone him."

"Rockwell—Kenneth Rockwell?" Wentworth pondered aloud, and into his mind flashed the image of a serious young scientist whom he had met on several occasions but knew only slightly. "I'll call him."

"Mr. Wentworth?" Rockwell's voice came anxiously, the moment Wentworth called his number. "I hate to bother you, but I need your help very badly. I am in trouble—or, that is, I feel I am. It is trouble that I'm afraid I can't handle alone—"

"What about the police?" Wentworth interrupted. "The police are there to handle trouble, you know."

"I can't call the police. I can't tell you why, but I can't go to them," Rockwell rushed on nervously.

"There may not actually be anything wrong, but I'm very much afraid there is—and to call the police might only make it worse. You are the only one I know who can help me, Mr. Wentworth. I know it is an imposition, but if you could only come here to my office...."

Rockwell was almost incoherent, and Wentworth readily detected the fear throbbing in his voice. The man seemed badly scared, on the verge of panic when Wentworth did not immediately agree to make the trip.

"It will only take an hour or two of your time—at the most," he begged. "I'll pay you—I'll pay *anything* that I am able, Mr. Wentworth. Please... while we are talking here the thing may happen. I am in my office in the Egyptian wing of the Consolidated Museum. *Please* come and let me tell you...."

Ordinarily, Wentworth would have refused such a vague plea. Nita's dinner party was infinitely more important than the panicky fears of a man who was almost a stranger to him. Yet, tonight he agreed—because a shriveled mummy hand seemed to be beckoning him and setting his nerves atingle.

THE CONSOLIDATED MUSEUM was dark when

Wentworth finally arrived at its front door. But a watchman was there to let him in, and even before the attendant had an opportunity to guide him to the office of the Egyptian department, Kenneth Rockwell came hurrying forward to meet him. The young fellow shook hands nervously, almost abstractedly, and started to lead the way back to his own wing of the big building.

"It is Sue Warrington, my fiancée, who has me so worried," he confided as they walked through the dimly lit exhibition rooms. "I believe you know her, Mr. Wentworth—the daughter of Austin Warrington, the explorer-scientist? I was with him on an expedition to the Gobi Desert. Sue disappeared two days ago, without a word to any of us. I became alarmed when nothing was heard of her by last night, but Mr. Warrington forbade me to report her disappearance to the police. He said it probably would turn out to be nothing—but I don't believe that, Mr. Wentworth! I don't believe he meant it, either. I am certain that he was afraid—terribly afraid of something he would not admit to me."

He went on. "Late this afternoon I received a message from Sue. How it came I don't know—it simply was here on my desk when I returned to the office from one of the exhibition rooms. Here it is." He took a small, penciled note from the drawer of his desk and handed it to Wentworth. "Sue wrote it, all right, there's no question about that. The handwriting is hers—and yet, somehow, the wording isn't. That's what makes me suspicious."

Wentworth stared down at the neatly written note:

Kennie dear:

I must see you! Please be in your office in the Consolidated this evening if you want to establish contact with me. *Please* do not fail me—if you ever want to see me again!

Your own,

"Susie Q"

"That's 'Kennie'—" Rockwell pointed out over Wentworth's shoulder—"Sue never called me that. She would have asked me to meet her in the 'museum,' not in the 'Consolidated'—and certainly she would not have misspelled the name. And that 'Susie Q' signature doesn't make sense—unless she was writing the note under duress, pretending to be signing a pet-name signature while, actually, *trying to warn me to be on my guard.* That is what I fear she was trying to do, trying to warn me about something. But what that might be, I don't—"

His low, tense voice echoed, unnaturally loud, in the stillness of the great empty building, then clipped off in mid-sentence as the office lights suddenly blinked out. For an instant, absolute silence gripped the darkened office that was now illuminated only dimly by the bluish radiance of an emergency light in the exhibition room just outside the glass door, and then something weird and unnatural came charging through the blue gloom.

Wentworth stared, his eyes dilating!

The incredible thing was a ghastly, shriveled mummy! From where it had come he had no idea, yet suddenly it was there in the office, was flinging itself upon Rockwell, bearing him back against the wall. Wentworth caught a glimpse of a ghastly, skeletal face as they pitched past the door, saw a bony arm raise and swing down at Rockwell with a vicious-looking knife that seemed to spark blue lightning as the pallid beam etched it.

Rockwell gasped, a strangled sound that blended amazement with terror, utter horror. For a moment it seemed that the descending knife must plunge into his throat. Then he had slipped clear, was backing away frantically, stumbling free and losing his balance. He was going down... but in that instant Wentworth flung himself across the office and clutched the horrible apparition, caught it around the knees in a football tackle. The withered legs were like sticks in his hand; the weight was almost nothing as it toppled forward and fell to the floor.

It had all happened in the flash of a second—Rockwell floundering and going down backward against one of the specimen cases that lined that side of the office, the grisly creature toppling headlong, and then the shattering crash as the specimen case overturned on top of it. In the next second Wentworth was scrambling to his feet, staring at Rockwell, who had gotten to his knees and now gaped like one stricken.

"God—oh, great God Almighty!" came almost tonelessly from Rockwell's lips as he stared at the over-turned case.

Then, like an automaton, he crept over to the wreckage and, on his knees, gaped down at the shocking face of the desiccated creature on the floor. The full weight of the heavy specimen case had come down on its chest, had crushed it in and flattened its snapped ribs, Wentworth lit a match, held it over the graveling. The glass cover had slapped across its forehead tearing away a large patch of skin—but not a drop of blood came from the shriveled flesh now laid bare by the wound!

But it was not this creepy phenomenon that held Rockwell's horror-stricken eyes. They were riveted on that ghastly face, on the sunken cheeks and cavernous eye sockets that stared up at him sightlessly. His lips moved soundlessly, and then Wentworth caught the half-whisper of his words.

"Sue—Sue," the name dribbled tonelessly from his mouth. "It's Sue Warrington—my Sue!"

"Snap out of it, man!" Wentworth clipped as he grabbed the young fellow by the shoulder, shook him. "You've had a shock—"

Yet when he lit another match he saw that Rockwell was not a victim of his own imagination. Perspiration was standing out on his forehead in great beads, running down his face as he crouched beside the brown-skinned skeleton.

"She is hardly recognizable," he said slowly, with the awful nearness of hysteria. "Hardly recognizable—but I know my Sue. The devil himself must have had her, Wentworth. What in God's name did he *do* to her?"

WHAT *had* happened to Sue Warrington? That question was throbbing through Richard Wentworth's brain as he stared, aghast, at the incredibly shriveled and withered corpse of what, only a few days before, had been a beautiful young woman. For two days she had been missing, and now to be returned to her fiancé like this—a crazed mummy bent on murdering him before the yawning grave closed forever over her....

A mummy!

That was it! Suddenly something clicked in Wentworth's brain, and the haunting half-memory that had been plaguing him ever since he talked with Wilbur Patterson took definite form. What he had been striving to recall was a brief news story that had appeared in one of the local papers a few days ago. He remembered now—it was in the *Chronicle*. A humorously treated account of someone who claimed to have seen a mummy running across a driveway in Central Park.

The writer, his tongue in his cheek, had intimated that the beholder of this remarkable sight had perhaps been slightly overstimulated. But there was no convenient alcoholic explanation for *this* ghastly mummy lying at his feet on the museum floor. This mummy was stark reality, and so might have been that one in the park. Wentworth knew he must at once learn more about that other emaciated prowler—and the likeliest source for information was the newsroom of the *Chronicle*.

He glanced at his watch. The *Chronicle* staff would be at work now, but he ought not to leave the museum until the police arrived. That would mean delay, questioning, an amazed and incredulous investigation—perhaps even a trip down to Headquarters. Precious moments, perhaps even hours, would be lost. He could not afford to lose that much time. Not only the solution of Sue Warrington's horrible death but another life might now be hanging in the balance.

"You will have to report this to the police, Rockwell." He made his decision as he drew the dazed man to his feet and led him to a desk chair. "I've got to run out on you for a while. Leave the body just as it is—that will be all the vindication you need. But should there be any difficulty, I will clear you."

Rockwell turned uncomprehending eyes to him. If he had heard, the words had not registered in his brain. But Wentworth had no more time for talk. The watchman may have heard the sound of the falling specimen case and might come to investigate at any moment.

Wentworth could have spared himself that last fear, he discovered as soon as he reached the front door. The old watchman sprawled there on the floor, blood trickling from a nasty gash in his scalp. Wentworth knelt beside him, saw that he was already recovering consciousness, and then was on his way.

JOHN GREGG, a thin, bald-headed man of dour mien, was the city editor of the *Chronicle*. Wentworth had met the newspaperman on other cases and had a nodding acquaintance with him. Gregg was in the slot at the city desk, when Wentworth arrived. He glanced up, his high forehead wrinkled in a questioning frown as he peered at the card Wentworth had dropped on the desk. Then the frown deepened, became a bleak scowl.

"Mummy story?" he echoed Wentworth's question almost belligerently. "What mummy story?"

"The man who saw a mummy in Central Park," Wentworth repeated.

"Oh, that stick we ran last Tuesday or Wednesday," Gregg deprecated. "Last Tuesday is ancient history in the newspaper business, my friend. How do you expect me to remember which one of my men plugged a hole in a column with a space-filler? The yarn was a pipe-dream—some young cub's inspiration, probably. Sorry that I can't help you. Here you, copy-boy!" and he busied himself with a sheaf of yellow copy paper that lay in front of him.

Wentworth eyed him narrowly before turning away. The man

was brusk to the point of being insulting, but his blustering acerbity had failed its purpose. Wentworth saw through it— and saw that John Gregg was a very badly frightened man. The moment he had heard the word "mummy" stark fear had flared in the editor's eyes, had almost popped his loose-lipped mouth wide open.

Fear—why?

There was no use questioning him, Wentworth realized. At best, Gregg would lie—if he did not take refuge in open incivility. But the editor's instant reaction had been no accident. In some way, it tied up with that grim tragedy in the Consolidated Museum….

Wentworth was walking downstairs thoughtfully on his way to the street when a freckled, broad-faced man of about twenty-five caught up with him. Wentworth felt the other's eyes upon him, turned to investigate.

"You're Richard Wentworth, aren't you?" The fellow grinned. "I'm Ted O'Neill—reporter upstairs. I remember you from the Black Police terror days—and when you're around I smell a yarn. You're interested in that mummy yarn, eh?" He paused and exhaled a cloud of smoke without removing the handmade cigarette from between his lips. "I wrote that story—and Gregg knows it," he said almost meditatively, the grin vanished. "I heard what he said to you. There's something damned queer about that—something that's been eating at Gregg the past couple days—"

"Do you remember the man who gave you that story?" Wentworth plumped at him.

"Yeah—I do." The reporter nodded. "He was on odd sort of jigger—that's why I ribbed him. But, funny thing about that, I had a queer hunch that he was telling the *truth*. His name is Maurice Somers, lives in a rooming-house on West Forty-ninth—three-ten, I think it was. I suppose you're going over there?" He eyed Wentworth shrewdly. "Okay, I'll tail along—might help to open him up a bit."

The front door of the rooming-house was open, and a slatternly-looking woman, who sat on the steps, told them that Somers lived on the third floor rear. She didn't know whether he was in, she admitted discouragingly—hadn't seen anything of him for two or three days.

Without comment they climbed to the third floor and located the room. But there was no response to their knock. Twice Wentworth repeated it—and then turned to O'Neill, a half-question in his eyes.

If they....

"Same here," the reporter agreed. "I'd like to get a squint behind that door. Maybe we ought to get the old dame to unlock it."

"That will mean a lot of questions and argument," Wentworth vetoed the suggestion, and out of his pocket came a self-adjusting skeleton key that slipped into the spring lock.

For a few moments he worked over it, manipulating it so that the tiny steel teeth moved into place to fit the grooves of the lock—then it turned and the door was open.

Cautiously he stepped inside, peering into the dark room…

and then he felt for the light cord, tugged it and snapped on the single baleful overhead bulb.

"My God!" burst from Ted O'Neill's lips, and the breath went out of him in an amazed gasp. He stood beside the iron-framed bed, gaping down at its grisly occupant. "That's him—Somers! It was him!"

Stretched out on the sheet was a gaunt skeleton clad only in a pair of shorts, the knobby bones tightly covered with the sear, brown skin of a mummy... A mummy from which both hands had been amputated at the wrists!

CHAPTER 2
HANDS OF DEATH

"MULLER, ONE of the cops on the Central Park beat, was talking to this fellow Somers when I came along—that was about eight o'clock last Monday night," Ted O'Neill outlined the genesis.

"Muller was kidding him—thought it was a big joke. But Somers was insistent about what he bad seen. He said that he had been dozing on a park bench. Right in front of him, running across the driveway, was a creature that looked like Mahatma Gandhi, only *more* so."

The reporter frowned. The thing had on nothing but a pair of shorts—like Somers had there now—and so skinny it looked like a mummy. It was running squarely at him, so he got a good look at it under the park light. Two men came tearing after it and caught it before it quite reached him. They picked it

RICHARD WENTWORTH

up, and thrust it into a sedan that came rolling up after them. He couldn't give much of a description of the men, but he did remember the sedan—a special-built Cadillac with a maroon body and light-gray trim. He noticed particularly that the right rear disk wheel was badly dented.

O'Neill puffed abstractedly on his omnipresent cigarette.

"That's what got me about his yarn, Wentworth. He described that car so completely that I felt he actually had seen something. But I never believed that he had seen *anything* like this...."

Wentworth had closed the door of Somers' room as soon as he glimpsed that travesty of a human figure on the bed. Swiftly he completed an examination of the dried-up corpse and then searched the barely furnished room while he listened to O'Neill. The search produced nothing to give the slightest hint as to how or why Somers had met his fate. But Wentworth's brain was spinning at top speed, flashing back to that other mummy he had seen little more than an hour ago.

Kenneth Rockwell had said that he had not reported Sue Warrington's disappearance to the police because her father had forbidden him to do so. Austin Warrington must have had a reason for keeping the news quiet—and Wentworth wanted very much to know what that reason was. Quickly he outlined to O'Neill the girl's strange disappearance and death.

"Two mummies in one night!" The reporter's lips pursed into a silent whistle. "Man, we *have* got something here! What's next—where are we headed for now?"

"To see Austin Warrington," Wentworth clipped, as he snapped off the light and locked the door on the emaciated body. "We'll report this later—but I want time before the police sound the alarm. You stay with me until I say the word, O'Neill—then you can have all the scoop you want."

"Will I?" Ted O'Neill grunted. "Just try to shake me!"

Fifteen minutes later a taxi delivered them in front of the old-fashioned brownstone building on East Thirty-sixth Street, near Park Avenue, that was the home of Austin Warrington. Wentworth led the way up the short flight of stone steps—and stopped in surprise when the door opened and Kenneth Rockwell came out.

"Hello, Wentworth," he greeted nervously. "I guess you're surprised to see me here. The truth is I have not yet reported Sue's death to the police. I'm afraid I have been sort of running around in circles. This thing came as such a shock... I didn't know just what to do after you left. So I came over here to tell Mr. Warrington what had happened and ask his advice. I found Carson, the watchman, half conscious from a blow on the head. He's all right now and is keeping guard at the museum."

Rockwell's patrician-featured, student's face was drawn and haggard. His mouth twitched and his lips quivered as he seemed to fight back his grief and struggle for self-control. Apparently the tragedy had unnerved him completely.

"I am going back now—to notify the police," he mumbled uncertainly as he continued down the steps. "Mr. Warrington says that I should have done that immediately. But... with the condition of her body... nobody will ever be able to tell...."

18

Wentworth watched him go, then rang the bell. Warrington's impassive-faced Chinese valet answered and took Wentworth's card. He returned promptly to usher the visitors into a spacious living-room where the retired scientist-explorer sat slumped in a massive leather easy-chair, his large head half-bowed as if its weight was too much for him to uphold.

"HOW DO you do, Mr. Wentworth?" he looked up, and Wentworth saw that his usually round face had lost its fullness; seemed to have sagged and become gaunt with horror. "Kenneth has told me that you tried to help him, but arrived too late. We appreciate what you did, nevertheless."

Wentworth noticed that his hands trembled as if he were suffering from ague; noticed that his whole body twitched and fairly writhed under the stress of his emotion.

"Sue was all that I had to live for," he said brokenly, miserably. "She was my whole life, and now she is dead—and it is my own fault. I could have prevented it, Mr. Wentworth, if only I had known…."

"You knew where she was, Mr. Warrington?" Wentworth probed gently. "You knew where she had been taken?"

"No." The large head shook wearily, "I did not know that—but I had been warned that something would happen. That was why I did not dare report my daughter's disappearance to the police—I was afraid she would be killed if I did. Several weeks ago, I received the first demand and threat over the telephone. Whoever it was, wanted a hundred thousand dollars. I laughed at him and hung up, but he called again a week later. That time he was more threatening. I hung up on him again."

He shuddered. "The third time he called, he told me that I was going to be taught a lesson. That was the day before Sue disappeared. The next day Wong found a package on the doorstep addressed to me, and that evening my daughter did not come home. The package contained this…."

Leaning forward, he opened a drawer of the center table and gingerly lifted out a mummified hand. A hand with a message burned into the dry brown skin on its back—*The reward of disobedience is death!*

Wentworth stared down at that grisly harbinger of doom—and the fingers of his hand, thrust into the pocket of his topcoat, touched the mate of that mute warning. The hand on Warrington's table was a right. Late that afternoon the left, which once had been its companion, had been placed on Wilbur Patterson's desk!

The left hand, and now the right—and this one had already signalized ghastly death for an innocent girl….

Promising Warrington that he would do everything possible to help bring Susan's murderer to justice, Wentworth got away as quickly as possible with O'Neill. Hurrying to the corner, he hailed a taxi. They were no more than seated inside when another passenger sprang onto the running-board. The fellow made no attempt to enter the cab; merely clung to the door and glued his body against the side.

It was a short, hunched-up figure… and then the passing illumination of an arc-light abruptly revealed its face. A sear mummy mask out of which wild, maniacal eyes glared with fanatical purpose. Just a flash of that horrible countenance… but it was sufficient to shout a warning of the assassin's deadly purpose.

Instantly, Wentworth leaped from the seat, trying desperately to pry loose those clutching fingers. But like steel vises they were clamped on the sides of the door. With all his strength Wentworth drove his fist into that gargoyle face—again and again. A whimper of agony was torn from between the battered lips, but the attacker seemed almost immune to punishment. Wentworth's fist smashed home, with such force that his arm tingled to the elbow—and at last that inhuman grappling-iron grip was broken.

With a strangled cry the assailant teetered on the running-board, lost his balance and fell backward—just as the stillness of the night was torn by a terrific explosion. The car rocked crazily under the concussion. It heeled up on one side and seemed about to turn over as it skidded halfway across the street.

"Geez—what in hell was that?" the scared driver chattered as he recovered control of the machine and jammed on the brakes.

But the answer to that question, Wentworth saw, as he peered back out of the rear window, would never be fully known. The attacker he had knocked off the running-board had practically disintegrated—blown into unrecognizable bits by the load of sudden death which must have been strapped to his body.

"Never mind stopping—there is nothing we can do," Wentworth ordered the cabbie. "Get us uptown."

SHAKEN BY that close brush with death, Wentworth sat back on the seat and tried to figure it all out while the cab sped northward. Had he and O'Neill been followed from the rooming-house where they had found Somers' mummified remains? Had the frenzied killer waited outside Austin Warrington's home, prepared to wipe out anyone who might come to the old man's aid? What other reason could there be for this attempt on their lives?

Suddenly into his mind flashed the memory of John Gregg's frightened eyes. Was it possible that Gregg had seen him leave the *Chronicle* office with Ted O'Neill, then had them followed and ambushed as they departed from the Warrington residence? That seemed too far-fetched, and yet Wentworth wondered a great deal....

"What did you mean about Gregg having something 'eating' him the past few days?" He turned to O'Neill.

"Eh?" the reporter started. "Phew—I was just thinking about that close call. If that bird had clung to this cab another half-minute we wouldn't be sitting here now worrying about mummies and John Gregg. Gregg? I don't know what has been the matter with him. He's been jumpy as a cat, ready to hop down anyone's throat with half an excuse. Once or twice I've seen him answer the phone and go white as a sheet before he put it down. But maybe that's only my imagination. Looking at mummies and hearing that talk of Warrington's is enough to give anyone ideas!"

He changed the subject. "What's this place we're headed for

now, Wentworth? East Sixty-fifth, just off the park—pretty swank neighborhood. Another mummy waiting for us there?"

He wasn't joking.

But before Wentworth could answer the cab turned off Madison Avenue into East Sixty-fifth Street, and O'Neill bounced upright and pressed close to the front window.

"You sure know how to put your finger on it!" he marveled. "Look at that—half the cops in New York!"

Wentworth's heart sank as he followed the reporter's gaze. A dozen radio cars were drawn up at the curbs, and the sidewalk in front of Wilbur Patterson's home fairly swarmed with blue uniforms. Among the machines he spotted Police Commissioner Stanley Kirkpatrick's car, with the department chauffeur sitting at the wheel.

Kirkpatrick was on hand, taking charge of the case personally. That meant something of unusual importance—something sensational. Tonight, Wentworth was certain, it meant murder. It meant that he was too late to save Wilbur Patterson's life....

WENTWORTH'S FEARS were fully realized as he was passed into the building by police officers who knew him. The commissioner, they told him, was upstairs "with the body"—but even before he and O'Neill reached the center of attention they saw plenty of evidence of what had occurred in that house. The place was turned topsy-turvy, Patterson's office ransacked, his books and papers tossed about in wild confusion.

His laboratory, behind the office, was the worst. It was utterly wrecked, and in the midst of his ransacked and plundered belongings lay the body of the inventor, his skull beaten to a pulp, his body horribly twisted and torn. Those vicious blows on the head had killed him... but not until he must have gone through untold agony in the hands of a merciless torturer!

Stanley Kirkpatrick, immaculate in evening clothes and with an ever-present gardenia on his jacket lapel, looked up from the gruesome sight on the floor. His saturnine face had lost some of its usual ruddy glow. Handsome, well-set-up, square-built, in his late forties, Kirkpatrick had devoted his whole life to police work. He was no stranger to violent death, yet the cold-blooded barbarity of the things that had been done to this helpless victim shocked him.

"It's horrible, Dick," he muttered as he caught sight of Wentworth. "One of the worst things I have ever seen. Poor Patterson must have gone through hell itself."

Only then did he realize that Wentworth's presence here was not altogether regulation—that this man, with whom he had faced so many baffling crimes, was not a member of the police department and had not been summoned to the scene of this outrage. Kirkpatrick's eyes widened with surprise, then narrowed in sudden suspicion.

"How is it you are *here* so promptly, Wentworth?" he snapped. "How did you know anything was wrong?"

Wentworth's eyes were steel-hard, his face bleak as he looked down at the battered corpse of the man who had been his friend. Patterson's jesting words were still ringing in his ears, and he hardly heard Kirkpatrick's voice—but Ted O'Neill heard.

"Another mummy murder—that's the answer!" the reporter

blurted as he stared down at the body. "Now I know why we came here—"

"A mummy murder— what's *that?*" Kirkpatrick caught him up quickly.

Too late the reporter tried to hold his tongue. Contritely he looked at Wentworth, but Wentworth shrugged.

"There will be another astounding murder waiting for you when you get back to headquarters, Kirk," he said quietly. "Sue Warrington. Some fiend got hold of her, drained off all her blood and turned her into a shrunken mummy. We have just come from having a talk with her father—and because we came right here O'Neill thinks I anticipated this."

"You came straight here from Warrington's." Kirkpatrick jumped at the first lead he had found. "That's no coincidence, Wentworth—you knew something about what was going on here, and I want to know what it is. You're coming down to headquarters with me now." Although it was said bluntly, he attempted a smile—but anxiety killed it.

"Is this an arrest, Commissioner?" Wentworth asked softly.

"No, it's not," Kirkpatrick snapped, and now his glance harassedly clashed with that of the man who was his best friend. "I don't want it to be an arrest, but, if you hold back material information, it will have to be."

Without a word, the two rode side by side in the back seat

of Kirkpatrick's car while O'Neill rushed back to the *Chronicle* office to pound out his scoop. It was not until Wentworth sat facing him across the big desk in Kirkpatrick's private office, that the commissioner again spoke.

"There is something afoot, Dick," he said earnestly. "I know that—and you know it. A man has been brutally murdered, his valet found the body and reported it to the police, my men responded and are working on the case—that is police business, nobody else's. If you have information that will help us solve this crime, it is your duty to turn it over. It is not your duty to constitute yourself as an extra-legal police force and take the law into your own hands."

He sighed. "We have been over this ground so many times. Often, I admit, the results you achieved may have justified your methods—but not this time. This is police business, pure and simple. We can handle it ourselves—and we don't need the help of the Spider."

Eye to eye they faced each other, the police commissioner of the City of New York and the man he was morally certain was that Nemesis of crime whose identity was hidden beneath the dark cloak of the Spider. Morally certain, but not legally so—for if ever Stanley Kirkpatrick came into possession of actual proof that his suspicions were correct there would be but one course open to him. Once he could prove that Richard Wentworth and the Spider were one, the warm friendship and deep regard he held for Wentworth would weigh nothing against his stern duty.

Once Kirkpatrick secured that proof, Wentworth knew that he would be arrested and turned over to the prosecutor. The electric chair would be the Spider's reward for the unorthodox way in which he settled those grievous wrongs which the Law could not rectify. Wentworth knew this, and he admired Stanley Kirkpatrick, his unimpeachable honesty—but was doubly careful that his friend should never have to face that grim duty.

Those thoughts flashed through his mind now as he looked into Kirkpatrick's earnest face.

"All right, Kirk," he capitulated. "I can't speak for the Spider, but I will keep hands off. Patterson called me in this afternoon, but he did not really ask me to help him. He thought this was a joke or a lunatic's prank," and Wentworth put the mummified hand on the commissioner's desk.

Quickly and thoroughly he outlined what he knew about Patterson's death, about Sue Warrington's strange fate, and about the mummified body of Maurice Somers. Kirkpatrick listened and his face became stern and hard, the fighting face of the police bulldog that he was.

"Another murdering lunatic," he snapped. "Thanks for your help, Dick—I appreciate it. I'll call you if there is anything else you can do for us—and now, good night."

DESPITE THE tragic events of the night, Wentworth could hardly restrain a smile as he walked out of police headquarters. Kirkpatrick had been so anxious to get rid of him; so fearful that the uncanny threat of this mummy death would act as a magnet to draw the Spider into the case.

But this, he was ready to admit, was police business. It was a case which really did not concern him, nor did it present a challenge such as the Spider would be bound to answer. With a feeling almost of virtue Richard Wentworth hailed a taxi and gave the driver the address of his Sutton Place apartment house.

Being with Evelyn Marlowe and Peter Hennessey at dinner that evening had had its effect upon him, too. Well he knew those secret desires which were deep in Nita's heart—desires which he shared completely. The peace and comfort of a home of their own, the happiness of life with her close at his side—he wanted to realize those dreams, too. But so long as his blood pounded, and his nerves tingled at the call of the criminal chase, he knew that those things were not for him.

So long as the Spider ruled his life, ready to respond at any moment to the call of those in trouble—those helpless ones who were being victimized by their lawless fellows in high and low places—he knew that he could offer Nita nothing more than the shell of a life she desired.

But perhaps he had reached the end of that period... Tonight he had been able to listen to Kirkpatrick, had been able to turn away resolutely and leave crime-fighting to the police. Perhaps at last....

The taxi had swung into Sutton Place and was approaching the apartment-house building which was one of the entrances by which Wentworth reached the stronghold that was located on the waterfront at its rear. He felt for his wallet—and suddenly his hand froze half-way to his hip. In that second his ever-watchful eyes had spied a car parked across the way from the building— and had identified it!

A maroon sedan with light-gray trim!

A special-built Cadillac, with the right rear disk wheel badly dented!

The car Maurice Somers had seen in Central Park!

Lithe and watchful, every nerve on trigger edge, Wentworth stepped out of the cab—to realize instantly that he was ambushed. Tongues of flame stabbed out at him from points on both sides of the car. Lead whistled by his head, slapped against the body of the cab, bored through its windshield. He was caught in the open, but two or three bounds would carry him to the shelter of the apartment entrance—which was exactly what these ambushers wanted him to do, intuition whispered the warning!

Instead, he threw himself back into the taxi, and then out through the other door. His twin automatics were clutched in tight fists as he bounded out onto the pavement and crouched beside the machine—his deadly guns lancing leaden slugs at those orange flashes.

One of the hidden marksmen screamed wildly as he vaulted to his feet then sprawled at full length in the gutter. Another howled in pain. A third cursed as he dropped his weapon clattering to the pavement and raced for the car across the street—only to pitch into it on his face as Wentworth's bullet caught him poised in the doorway.

Quickly Wentworth whirled back to face the others, and at that moment was knocked flat on the street as if a giant hand had slapped him down. All the world seemed to dissolve in a burst of blinding flame and a tremendous clap of ear-splitting thunder.

Half-stunned, Wentworth climbed to his knees on the running-board and saw that the whole front of the apartment building was wrecked, the entrance completely blown away. He realized what had happened. The chauffeur was no longer in the cab, was nowhere to be seen. Terrified by the gunfire, he had leaped from his seat and dashed into the building entrance—and had thus set off the deadly trap into which the killers had intended to herd Wentworth.

In that perilous moment Wentworth remembered the young fellow's pleasant smile and stared with bleak eyes at the photographs of the two youngsters pasted on the dashboard....

Grimly he staggered to his feet and propped his shoulders against the cab as he emptied his guns after the fleeing murder car. The tail-lights blinked out around a corner, and a strangely heavy silence, that seemed to be striving to blot out the last vestige of that fearful din, settled over the street.

Uncertainly Wentworth walked over to where the killer he had dropped into the gutter, still sprawled grotesquely. The fellow's hat had fallen off his black-thatched head, and his swarthy face was turned up to the dark sky. It was Enzo Nairn, a thug who had long been associated with a mob bossed by Patsy DeLott, one of the East Side's most powerful gang overlords.

Patsy DeLott—and it was into one of his cars that the Central Park mummy had been snatched....

Now he knew!

CHAPTER 3
THE HIDDEN GUEST

T HE SOUND of opening windows, the shrill scream of a frightened woman and then a man's shout snapped Richard Wentworth out of his reflections. Quickly he darted across the sidewalk, into the shadow of the buildings. Before the first curious investigators arrived he had disappeared around the corner and was negotiating another entrance to the place that to him was both home and stronghold.

The dazed stupefaction, that had momentarily glazed his eyes, was now replaced by a grim tightness of the jaws that brought out the muscles in hard little ridges below his cheeks.

Wanton, cold-blooded murder! A few minutes ago that smiling young taxi-driver had been getting ready to make change, to pocket another fare to go to the support of those kiddies whose photo traveled with him on all his hacking rounds. Now he was a battered pulp beneath a ton of fallen masonry!

Wentworth's fists clenched, and hot rage welled up in his heart. An innocent man murdered and his family left to starve, simply because he happened to be in the way when Patsy DeLott's killers were ready to spring their trap. This was police business, yes—but it was the business of the Spider, also! It was the business of the police to prevent tragedies of that sort. When they failed so completely that a man like DeLott could order around his deadly pawns with impunity, then it was the Spider's business to see that justice was done!

The murder of Wilbur Patterson he could have left to the

police, as he had promised. But to see arrogant criminals running roughshod over inoffensive and helpless bystanders was something Wentworth could not tolerate. The picture of those fatherless youngsters had touched his great heart and now goaded him to action like a flaming brand.

Patsy DeLott… it was from his nest that murder crew had come. Wentworth knew where that nest was located—the political clubhouse that was DeLott's hangout. That was where the mobster would be tonight—where he would wait to hear that his underlings had carried out their orders. And that was where

The terrified chauffeur had set off the deadly trap intended for Wentworth!

he would now render the accounting which he little suspected
was on the schedule....

Before the police arrived and closed off the vicinity of the
bombed building on Sutton Place, a dark sedan rolled out of one
of a row of private garages on a side street of that block. Unhin-
dered, it passed half a dozen sirening radio cars as it bore east-

ward. Then it turned to the south and streaked toward that part of the city where men like Patsy DeLott recruit their following from the close-packed hotbeds of crime.

On a side street deep in that section where Manhattan Island bulges over toward Brooklyn, Wentworth parked the car and walked a few doors to the avenue corner. It was well after midnight, but this block was not yet asleep. Lights shone brightly in a pool parlor that occupied the street floor of a building midway to the next corner. They also gleamed behind the plate-glass windows that fronted the second story of that building, beneath the spreading crest of a national political party.

This four-story structure was Patsy DeLott's stronghold. From the ostensibly independent pool parlor on the first floor to the "private" club-rooms at the top, he controlled it and everyone who came into it. In this building untold deviltry had been hatched.

Wentworth approached the building, passed it. Two doors beyond, he turned into a shabby doorway, opened the unlocked door and entered an evil-smelling hallway. Three flights of creaking stairs brought him to the top floor, and from there a rickety ladder led up to the roof scuttle. He negotiated it without interference, closed the scuttle behind him, and catfooted cross-roofs to DeLott's.

A fire-escape in the rear led down to a patch of back yard, but Wentworth wanted none of that. Crossing to the farther end of the roof, he stopped above a row of windows that were not reached by the rusty iron structure. From beneath his vest came a length of stout rope, which he secured to a chimney and lowered over the edge of the roof. Then, for long minutes, he perched there beside the cornice while his fingers worked busily on his face—while secreted garments came out from inside his clothing and were donned, one after the other....

SATISFIED AT last, he lowered himself carefully over the edge—one floor, then another. At the second from the top he swung himself gently until he could gain a purchase for his feet on the window ledge, brace his hands on both sides of the frame and steady himself. This window, he knew, was in one of those private rooms where high-stake card games sometimes ran for days—where the loot of many a robbery had been tabled for division.

The window was dark now, and when he tested it cautiously he found that it was not locked. Noiselessly, he opened it and stepped inside—then out into the hallway, which was dark and deserted. Patsy DeLott's own rooms were on the floor below.

Carefully he tiptoed down the stairs. He gave silent thanks for the times he had been in this building and conferred with DeLott in a guise the gangster-politician never even thought to connect with Richard Wentworth.

There were half a dozen loungers in the main clubroom at the front of the building, Wentworth could see, when he reached the second floor. A low mumble of voices also came from the partly open doorway of DeLott's office, midway down the hall. Between was a little room that served as a kitchen for impromptu spreads, and beyond the politician's office, on the other side of the hall, was a lavatory.

As he picked his way down those stairs, Wentworth's brain

had been busily planning. Stepping across the hall, he opened the kitchen door and let himself inside. As he expected, there was a quantity of litter in a box beneath a pantry table—newspapers, old paper sacks, napkins and food containers. Piling them in the middle of the box, he set a match to the heap but blew out the blaze before it became dangerous. The charred bits were smoking lustily when he stepped out into the hall, leaving the door open behind him, and darted across to the lavatory.

Smoke was billowing out into the hall as he crouched behind the lavatory door. Thicker and thicker... and then flame.

Simultaneously with that flash, Patsy DeLott came striding from his office, sniffing the air suspiciously. Loosing an angry bellow, he charged the kitchen the moment he saw the flames. After him ran the half dozen henchmen with whom he had been conferring—leaving the way from the lavatory to the office clear.

"Damn careless fools!" DeLott roared. "I told 'em this would happen some day. They keep this place like a pigsty."

Panting and puffing with anger, his beefy face and thick neck crimson, he strode back into his office when the fire was extinguished. Impatiently he glanced at his watch as the others filed in after him and took seats in a semi-circle around the table over which he presided.

Footsteps sounded on the stairs, and into the office filed four crestfallen, glum-looking men. One of them had his right arm bandaged and in a sling.

"Well?" the boss gritted.

"I—I don't think we got him," he of the shifty eyes admitted.

"You don't *think!*" DeLott roared. "Since when can't you

tell when a punk is dead, Magnozzi? Oreste"—he glanced commendingly to a cold-eyed killer who sat at the far end of the table—"met you and gave you the stuff he got

from Patterson's place—enough to blow a dozen Wentworths into mincemeat. You were up there before the dude left police headquarters. There was plenty of time to plant it—so what?"

"We planted the stuff, all right—had everything ready...."

"And then let a damn fool taxi driver run in and blow himself to hell," the wounded man spat disgustedly. "Maggie did a fine job," he sneered. "Instead of plugging that hackie right off, he lets him get clear to gum the works. Ask him where Tony Slicci and Enzo Naldi are."

DeLott's eyes became pools of frenzy. They bored into Magnozzi's, threatened to drill them with sheer ferocity as he roared abuse at the leader of the luckless murder mission.

"I get it—Tony and Enzo are dead," he gritted. "You fell down, Magnozzi. You let that skunk Wentworth slip through your fingers, you lost two of my men!"

He rose, towering over his erstwhile lieutenant. His big hands opened and closed as if they would tear the blunderer to pieces; the veins stood out like whipcord at his temples and throat. But that show of rage did not fool one pair of keen eyes that was watching his every move. Patsy DeLott was afraid, and Wentworth knew it.

"You fell down!" he rasped again, and now an automatic clutched in his white-knuckled fingers, was trained on Magnozzi's belly. "You know damn well how I deal with bunglers. Get up—over across the room!"

But Magnozzi dropped back into his chair and cowered there abjectly as his eyes fixed fearfully on a door in the opposite wall.

That door, Wentworth knew, led to DeLott's private settlement room—room with soundproof steel walls and without windows. It was his execution chamber.

Magnozzi was a yellow coward, that was apparent—and yet there was something unnatural about his abject display. He seemed to be afraid of something more terrifying than death….

"Grab him!" DeLott spat an order to the others. "Drag him over there, if the yellow rat ain't got the guts to walk."

Two of them seized Magnozzi and dragged him to the door despite his frantic struggles and blubbering pleas for mercy. DeLott turned the key in the lock, threw the portal wide. Headfirst, the condemned man was thrown into the execution chamber—and in that moment the Spider went into action.

With a weird, discordant cackle that rang out above Magnozzi's howls, he sprang from the side closet in which DeLott had so often stationed his ready-triggered killers. A twisted, stooping figure in a long black cape and a wide, floppy-brimmed black hat that was pulled down low over a mop of thickly matted black hair and an incredibly ugly face.

Frozen with horror, those thugs turned to gaze into glittering eyes that leered at them from above a hooked nose and a jagged-toothed, lipless mouth. The wild cackle that issued from that fearsome creature rang in their ears like the knell of doom—

then was drowned in the roar of his flaming automatics.

Relentlessly the Spider dealt his stern justice—and the first to fall beneath his deadly fire was Oreste, the killer who had rifled Wilbur Patterson's laboratory.

"The Spider!" one of the terrified mobsters shouted fear-ridden recognition, and that dread name added to the panic. But like cornered rats they turned and flung at their Nemesis fiercely, with guns and knives, with chairs and anything that came to their hands.

Death sought him from every corner of that room, but the Spider danced a dizzy rigadoon that seemed to weave a magic way amongst them. Harmlessly their bullets thudded into the walls, their flung chairs smashed into kindling, and the overturned table came down only on their own luckless fellows. Straight for DeLott, the Spider marched, only to see the politician dive down and apparently evaporate into thin air.

A secret panel, of course, Wentworth cursed softly. DeLott had missed no bet in equipping this office for every emergency. But his desertion completed the rout of his henchmen. With howls of terror they dived for the door, fought one another furiously in their frenzied efforts to escape.

IN A few minutes it was over. The room still rang with the thunder of barking guns, the air was still acrid with the fumes of burned powder—but the Spider was the only one on his feet. For a moment he crouched there, ready for the first sign of renewed hostilities. Then he stooped over the body of the man Oreste, to press the bottom of his cigarette-lighter against the forehead of the dead killer—to stamp the corpse indelibly with a crimson replica of the insect from which he took his name.

DeLott's office was free of gangsters, but outside, in the hall and in the other rooms, Wentworth could hear the mob gathering, could hear them shouting directions, could hear their feet pounding on the stairs. They were organizing, preparing a trap for him. Every second counted now—but the closed door of that execution room drew him irresistibly.

Turning the key in the lock, he grasped the knob—and the door flew open as if a released spring were behind it. Out of the dark interior catapulted a frenzied thing of wildly flailing arms and legs, a maniacal thing that sniveled and whined like a tortured beast. Before he could back away, Wentworth's hands were full, had all that he could do to fight clear of what he now realized was a madman.

Magnozzi's brain had snapped under the terror of whatever that dark room contained. Now he was a terrified animal, a snarling, tearing beast that fought blindly and recklessly—but with prodigious strength.

Twice Wentworth managed to tear those clutching fingers away from his throat just in time to save his windpipe. Then the maniac was on him again, was bearing him backward, carrying him to the floor and swarming all over him. Desperately Wentworth tore his automatic free and clubbed it down on the madman's skull—again and again—until the killer's eyes widened like saucers, then closed as he tumbled in an inert heap.

No need to feel his heart to know that the man was dead. Bending over the bloody head, Wentworth pressed the brand of the Spider against the sweat-bathed forehead—a warning to Patsy DeLott and all his kind that not even an inconsequential taxi-driver could be slaughtered with impunity.

Leaping clear of the corpse, Wentworth sprang into the room beyond, lighting the way with his pocket flash—and stopped short when its beam fell on two ghastly-looking figures that sat facing the door. Two hollow-eyed, shriveled mummy skeletons propped up in chairs. Two underworld denizens, by their dress and what was left of their appearance. Two of Patsy DeLott's mobsters who had failed to carry out his orders!

So that was the secret of the withering death which he had encountered twice before that night—a fearful weapon, a terrifying club, which Patsy DeLott wielded over the heads of his intended victims.

For a fraction of a second Wentworth hesitated there, and then he stooped over one of those gruesome creatures. Lifting it, he was surprised at its lightness—not more than twenty-five or thirty pounds. It was a burden that he could cradle beneath his left arm.

The door leading from DeLott's office to the hall was closed, and even before he touched the knob he knew that it was locked. But there was another door, one leading to a short corridor that ran behind the kitchen and then into the main clubroom. It opened when he tried it—and Wentworth knew that that was where they would be waiting for him. But he had no choice—there was no other way out of that trap.

With the loathsome withered cadaver under his arm, the tight-skinned skeleton head grinning out in front of him only a little below his own, he stepped into that corridor and padded toward its farther end.

They were there, waiting for him in the darkened clubroom, the only light a single globe in the top of the corridor archway beneath which he would have to pass. Wentworth crouched and tensed every muscle.

With a blood-curdling scream he charged, ducking and diving fantastically with his macabre companion.

The moment he reached that archway a blinding flash lit up the whole clubroom like noonday, and the walls fairly rocked with the thunder of gunfire. Lead blasted at him, pocked the walls where he had been a split-second before—but almost instantly it was stilled. Instead of the din of pistol fire the big clubroom was filled with the frantic rush and clatter of feet as the panic-stricken mobsters dived for cover and shied away from those charging horrors.

His guns blazing right and left, the Spider slashed his way through them—and they could not get out of his path fast enough.

Straight through that clubroom and down the stairs he marched. One glimpse of the leering head of the mummy was all that was needed to clear the hall door of the poolroom—

and then he was out on the street, was racing to his car with his horrid burden.

Wentworth glanced back as he flung himself behind the wheel and trod the starter. But there was no attempt at pursuit. Patsy DeLott's gun-brave hoods were in mortal terror.

CHAPTER 4
DEATH SCOOP

RICHARD WENTWORTH stood at the wide window of the capacious living-room on the third floor of the fortress-mansion that was his home, his gloom-shadowed eyes abstractedly watching the lazy East River traffic that passed below him. The morning was so quiet, so peaceful, that the thought of sudden death, of weird, diabolical doom, seemed utterly incongruous. Looking out over that workaday river it was hard to believe that eerie death festered on its bank; that an implacable war raged in the canyons of the city beside it. And yet there was a war, savage and more barbaric than any fought under military direction—a war of jackals on defenseless sheep.

Like modern bandit nations, Patsy DeLott had started hostilities without a declaration, had leaped without warning on his unsuspecting victims. But now the Spider had flung down his challenge, had stamped his kill and brought DeLott out into the open.

Now DeLott knew that his tie-up with the mummy deaths was no longer a secret—that at last there was one man in the city who could prove his connection with the criminal empire he dominated. While that man lived there was no safety for Patsy DeLott. Now his every resource, all of his ruthless power, would be brought to bear on the task of killing the Spider—and of wiping out Richard Wentworth, who had miraculously escaped the killers commissioned to dispatch him.

Wilbur Patterson, it seemed, had signed his own death-warrant when he called Wentworth instead of complying with the extortion demands that had been made upon him. By answering that call Wentworth had added himself to the list of those who must be removed. Two ruthless attempts against his life in one evening demonstrated how urgently his removal was desired.

That display of savagery indicated, too, that Kenneth Rockwell and Austin Warrington, with whom he had been in contact, were in the gravest of danger. The aura of peril also would extend over all those close and dear to him—to the faithful servants here in this building, and to Nita van Sloan.

The spark in the depths of Wentworth's eyes kindled and blazed hotly. His fine athlete's shoulders squared, and his tall figure balanced there on the balls of his feet, his jaw hard and fists clenched behind his back.

The moment he crossed purposes with these underworld rats, it was Nita who would be placed in greatest jeopardy. He had already telephoned to remind her that she had an early engagement with him that morning at Sutton Place—which was all the warning Nita van Sloan would need. But that message would already have set her to worrying, to eating out her heart with fear for him....

"Your pardon, *sahib*," a deep, nasal voice interrupted, as a bearded and turbaned Hindu appeared in the doorway. "The *missie sahib* is here."

"Very well, Ram Singh," Wentworth nodded. "Call Jackson and Jenkyns and come back yourself. It is time that we talk."

Nita van Sloan's lovely face was a shade paler than usual, her violet eyes a degree darker as they studied Wentworth's face. Jackson, who had served with him in the trenches of France, was almost as poker-faced as his chief, stoically waiting to hear what was required of him. Jenkyns, the old butler who had served Wentworth's father before him, was obsequious, almost apologetic for his presence in this war council where he seemed so out of place. And Ram Singh, the tall Hindu descendant of a long line of Indian warriors, gently fingered the haft of his knife.

Quickly Wentworth acquainted them with what had occurred.

"We have no choice now," he finished. "We are undoubtedly marked for elimination—unless we eliminate Patsy DeLott first. Rockwell and Warrington are in constant danger. Jackson, I want you to keep watch on Warrington's place and let me know anything of importance that happens there. Jenkyns, you will take your station at the private wire behind the garage and act as liaison for the rest of us. Ram Singh, to you I am entrusting the safety of the *missie sahib*.

"That leaves only young Rockwell, and I have already engaged Mike Fogarty to look after him—"

The clamor of the telephone cut him short.

"Kirkpatrick," he told them with a tight half-grin as he

· *NITA VAN SLOAN* ·

dropped the receiver back into its cradle. "It seems my presence is desired down at headquarters."

JUDGED BY the baleful glance with which Stanley Kirkpatrick greeted him, Richard Wentworth's presence was anything but desired at police headquarters. Kirkpatrick sat back in his chair.

"I thought you were going to keep out of this, Dick," he blurted. "You gave me your word—and then you walked out of here and deliberately broke it. I told you that we did not need the help of the Spider. We can handle our business without employing murder. That's what that was in Patsy DeLott's clubhouse last night—deliberate, defiant murder!"

"I read in this morning's paper that there was some sort of disturbance in DeLott's place," Wentworth said quietly, when the fuming commissioner stopped to catch his breath. "Two of his men killed—"

"And arrogantly stamped with the seal of the Spider!" Kirkpatrick amended.

"The trouble with that stamp is that anyone can use it," Wentworth observed. "If I wanted a cover-up for a crime, I can't think of a better—"

He stopped.

"I know I can't pin a thing on you, Dick," Kirkpatrick leaned forward and nervously patted his flattened hand on the top of his desk. "Not yet—but if I lay hands on the evidence I need, I'll clap you into jail instantly. No man is higher than the law, and no man is infallible—not even the Spider."

He continued. "Patsy DeLott may be your solution to these mummy crimes—but you are wrong; entirely wrong." He said this emphatically. "This morning my men have brought in three

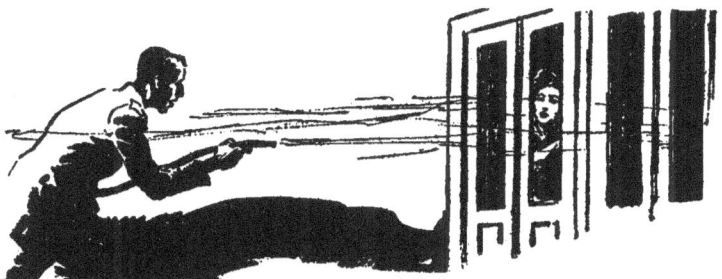

more mummified corpses, and two of the wealthiest men in this town have appealed to me for protection after receiving these severed hands. These were cases where DeLott and his cheap thugs could not possibly have penetrated—I have checked that thoroughly."

He frowned. "This mummy scare is the work of a criminal far more clever than DeLott—and I already have my suspicions of that criminal's identity. The best department surgeons worked over the corpses of Somers and the Warrington girl most of last night. The thing stumps them, they admit. Their only conclusion is that the mummifying must have been accomplished by the use of some little known embalming fluid—perhaps a drug of the sort the ancient Egyptians used. Does that suggest anything to you, Dick?"

He demanded suddenly, "What do you know about this chap Rockwell? He is a recognized authority on Egyptology, a highly esteemed student of ancient lore—I've checked that. What else do you know about him? Nothing. Suppose he decided to commit murder. What better alibi could he have than to get Richard Wentworth down there in his office as an eye witness when his crazed victim was released and killed? And he did kill her, accident or not—don't forget that."

"But how about the watchman?" Wentworth mused. "He was all right when he admitted me, but knocked out when I left. Rockwell would have had no chance to do that."

"An accomplice," Kirkpatrick snapped. "He could not handle this thing alone. I am making no charges against him, understand—but Mr. Kenneth Rockwell is a lead that will be thoroughly investigated. That's all, Dick." The commissioner swung back to his desk. "I called you down here to warn you. The Spider is going to keep out of this case, and if he doesn't—if he commits one more act of violence—I am going to take the bull by the horns and clap you in jail!"

THAT WAS braggadocio, Wentworth realized, as he left headquarters and started uptown. Kirkpatrick had let his anger run away with him, and that was an index of his anxiety. The commissioner was worried, badly worried, by this weird menace now reaching out for the city's wealthiest citizens. The fact that the doctors were unable to aid him undoubtedly added greatly to his concern. Once that fact became public property Wentworth could visualize the panic it would create—but before then he hoped to have run down the secret of the withering death.

Preparations for that he had started last night when he drove his mummy companion to the home of Dr. Rogers, an expert physician who was always more than anxious to do all in his power to repay Wentworth for past favors. Rogers had stared at the emaciated body in amazement and then tackled the problem with a will. If anyone could discover what had happened to the victim, Wentworth was convinced that the physician could do it. Yet now, when he was ushered into the office of Rogers' private sanitarium, the doctor greeted him with a dubious head shake.

"Bad as that, Doc?" Wentworth grinned.

"Worse," Rogers admitted. "I have been with your playmate almost constantly since you brought him here, Wentworth— but I know about as much as I did before I started. All my tests have failed. It is incredible that a human body could be aged so quickly—unless whoever did it employed drugs which are unknown to modern medicine. You have come just in time. I've received another batch of chemicals I want to try. Give me a hand."

Wentworth went into the laboratory with him and watched as the desiccated limbs of the mummy were treated in one bath after another; as the wasted tissues were dissected and examined with the latest scientific equipment. All afternoon they worked, and when they were finished the result was—complete failure.

"I am licked," Rogers swore, as he stripped off his rubber gloves and flung them on the porcelain table beside the weirdly wasted corpse. "I can't do anything more, Wentworth. There is only one thing I can suggest. If any man in America can solve this riddle he is Orrin Castleman, out at Leland Stanford. If you can induce him to come here—"

"Handle it for me, Doctor," Wentworth directed. "Send him a wire. Offer him anything he asks. The main thing is speed. We want him right away. Tell him to come by plane."

Rogers got busy immediately, and before night was able to phone Wentworth that the specialist would take a plane for New York in the morning. Perhaps Castleman would be the solution, Wentworth considered as he replaced the phone in its holder. At least he was a possibility—

And then Jenkyns was buzzing again.

"Hello, Mr. Wentworth—this is O'Neill, the *Chronicle*," came over the wire as soon as he lifted the receiver. "I've got to see you—quick. I'm at the office—and can't get away. I can't say any more over the phone, but get this—hell will be popping in another hour unless you can find some way to stop it. Come down here as fast as you can make it. I'll watch for you."

BEFORE WENTWORTH could reply the call snapped off. He made no attempt to reestablish it. The suppressed excitement in Ted O'Neill's voice had been even more eloquent than his words.

Hurrying down to the row of garages which bordered one side of his property, Wentworth got into a speedy coupé and headed for the downtown office of the *Chronicle.*

Ted O'Neill… Thinking of the reporter reminded Wentworth of their close escape from death the night before. That astonishing attack had not ceased to puzzle him, and again his mind tore at it, tried to figure what could have been behind it.

It could have been instigated by a number of people. But if Kirkpatrick knew the circumstances he, no doubt, would lay the blame at Kenneth Rockwell's door. True, Rockwell had seen Wentworth and O'Neill entering the Warrington house. If, as Kirkpatrick suggested, Rockwell was behind the mummy killings, he might have taken fright at Wentworth's activity in the case, might have quickly detailed a killer to waylay and do away with him—but that was too far-fetched to make sense.

Wentworth had dismissed it even before he drove up in front of the newspaper office and parked in back of an expensive-looking limousine. A low-number license plate—someone of importance, his subconscious clicked. Someone who employed an Oriental chauffeur, for he saw the bland-faced driver lounging behind the wheel.

BEFORE HE had reached the city room, Ted O'Neill met

him, took his arm and urged him down the hall. "Gregg is on both our necks, good and proper." The reporter grimaced. "He's been riding me all afternoon—probably would have canned me if it wasn't that my mummy scoop had it over the whole town. He's been secretive as hell all day, and just before I called you I found out why. You're it. Here—take a look at this."

Unfolding an ink-smeared stone-proof of the first page of the *Chronicle,* he handed it over—and Wentworth stared at a heavy black headline that sent a cold chill down his spine.

THE SPIDER IDENTIFIED
AS RICHARD WENTWORTH!

Beneath that startling announcement was a double-column story of the raid of Patsy DeLott's clubhouse, and next to that a blank space where a large, three-column picture was obviously to be inserted.

"Here's what goes in the center," O'Neill offered an engraver's proof of the cut—and Wentworth felt his skin prickling.

That picture was a photograph of the Spider with that ghastly mummy beneath his left arm—a photograph that must have been taken just as he charged into the front clubroom where DeLott's thugs were waiting for him. And then he remembered that blinding flash of light....

It had done its work excellently. The photograph was a hideous thing, the leering face of the mummy almost beside the Spider's ugly visage—but that was not all. That photograph had been cleverly doctored; retouched so that the Spider's face bore an unmistakable resemblance to Wentworth's own!

"This is to be a surprise edition," O'Neill was saying. "Gregg handled the whole thing himself. It's on the press now—that means it will be on the streets in a quarter of an hour. I don't know what's behind all this, Wentworth, but I can tell a doctored photo when I see one. You gave me a break last night, so I figured you had this much coming to you."

Once that edition reached the street Stanley Kirkpatrick would have the evidence he had been seeking—although secretly hoping *not* to find—all these years! Once it appeared, Wentworth would be definitely branded as the Spider, and Kirkpatrick would have no choice but to order his arrest, no matter what his own wishes might be!

The edition had to be stopped somehow... but how?

"What chance have I to get in to have a word with Gregg?" Wentworth asked as the possibilities flashed through his mind.

"None," O'Neill ended that hope.

"He's had two strong-arm men parked behind his chair ever since he came in—probably just waiting for you to try that."

Strong-arm men or not, that edition must be stopped. Yet Wentworth realized the futility of trying to reach the city editor by a direct assault. There must be some other way that would take Gregg unawares.

"How about the managing editor—is he in now?" Wentworth hazarded.

O'Neill glanced at his watch. "He should be. You ought to have seen his limousine and his Chink chauffeur down in front, if he is."

"Good enough," Wentworth clipped. "What's his name—and where is his office? I think I can make him see reason."

"Henry Mallon's his name," O'Neill answered dubiously, as he led the way down another corridor that branched off from the newsroom. "He's a pretty tough customer to argue with."

"I'll take a chance with him." Wentworth grinned. "Stay around in this corridor if you can. I'll let you know if I get any action."

With a show of confidence he opened the door and stepped inside—and breathed easier when he saw that Mallon's secretary's desk was empty. The managing editor was alone in the office, glancing over a sheaf of press-proofs that lay spread on his desk. He looked up in surprise, and then the color ebbed from round cheeks.

He was looking into the muzzles of a pair of automatics—a pair of automatics in the hands of Richard Wentworth, whom the *Chronicle* was exposing as a desperate criminal, the most notorious in New York's history—a man to whom human life meant nothing!

Mallon tried to speak, but when his lips opened his tongue clove to the roof of his mouth. He tried to turn his celebrated frigid stare on the intruder—but his eyes could not leave those black muzzles.

"You're not going to be hurt, Mallon," Wentworth assured him softly. "Not at all—if you are sensible and do what you are told. First of all, you are going to call John Gregg here to your office. Then you are going to step over into that wardrobe and be very quiet there. I am not going to gag or bind you—that isn't necessary with a man of your intelligence. But if you try to attract attention or create a disturbance—well, it will be extremely unwise."

The gun muzzles were very close to Mallon now, were moving behind him, on a level with his head. He could fairly feel them boring into his skull. Like a statue he sat there.

"First we want Gregg. Call him, Mallon," rang softly in his ears; and his arm reached out automatically for the phone.

"Gregg… Mallon speaking. I want to see you here in the office," he heard his voice saying.

"Alone," came from behind him.

"Alone," Mallon repeated, and put the receiver back on its hook.

"Now the wardrobe," Wentworth reminded.

Mallon walked across the office and stepped through the door into the dark closet, where at least those relentless gun muzzles would not be trained on him….

WENTWORTH WAS behind the door when John Gregg entered and glanced around uncertainly—was at the city editor's side before his jaw had a chance to drop open. The automatics were against Gregg's ribs, backing him toward Mallon's desk—but it was the look in Wentworth's eyes that made the newspaperman turn a sickly green.

"That's right, Gregg," Wentworth's words came softly, but the cold steel beneath them made the man shiver. "We are going to do some hurried editing. You know it would never do to have the *Chronicle* appear with that faked photo."

"I didn't know," Gregg gasped hoarsely. "I thought it was genuine—I had no reason for believing otherwise."

"Not when your photograph came from such an unimpeachable source," Wentworth agreed bitingly. "But there will be plenty of time to discuss that, Gregg. We're going off by ourselves to have a nice quiet talk, just you and I, in a little while—but first you are going to kill that edition before it reaches the street. Pick up that phone and call the pressroom. Have the presses stopped and the edition held before a copy goes out."

Those barked commands snapped at Gregg like a lash, and he cringed beneath them. Obediently he called the pressroom and gave the necessary orders, while beads of perspiration trickled down his forehead.

"Now remake that first page—in a hurry," Wentworth snapped. "A new streamer head, a new lead story, a box feature for the space where you intended to run that lying photo."

Gregg worked with frantic speed, cutting, pasting, remaking the new first-page.

"Now I am calling young O'Neill in here and you are giving him this to take to the composing room, the proofs to come back here to you," Wentworth outlined crisply. "My guns will be in my pockets—" his voice raised so that there would be no doubt of it penetrating the wardrobe.

Watchfully he went to the door and signaled O'Neill, who loitered half-way down the corridor. O'Neill responded with alacrity. Curiously he glanced around the office and at his waxen-faced superior. But John Gregg did as he had been told, and not a sound came from the wardrobe.

Wentworth breathed a fervent sigh of relief as the door closed behind the young reporter. So far, so good. He had stopped that damning edition.

The minutes went by. Gregg sat in his chair, glaring his hate.

Stillness… until suddenly there was the pound of running feet in the corridor, the sounds of a scuffle, a half-smothered yell. Instantly Wentworth was at the door, opening it a trifle.

O'Neill was out there in the corridor, struggling with two husky gorillas. One of them slammed him back against the wall, and the other closed in with a vicious uppercut—only to groan and drop in a heap as Wentworth's automatic came down over his skull. One smashing blow—and then the weapon caught the other.

"They are Gregg's strong-arm boys," O'Neill panted. "They got suspicious and followed me."

But Wentworth was already sprinting back to Mallon's office, prepared to see Gregg frantically phoning for help. He flung the door open—but Gregg was not near the telephone. He was sitting there at Mallon's desk as he had been, his head slumped over on his chest.

John Gregg was dead. His torso had been slit from stomach to throat, a deep, sweeping cut that had practically disemboweled him—and on the side of his forehead a brand had been burned… *the seal of the Spider!*

THAT MUCH Wentworth saw, and then he was springing past goggle-eyed O'Neill, leaping across, the office to an open window. There was a wide ledge outside that window, but it was empty, and so was the street below. At the curb stood Henry

Mallon's limousine, the Chinese chauffeur pacing up and down beside it—but there was no sign of a fleeing murderer.

Then the killer must still be there in the office. Wentworth whirled—and the muzzle of a weapon dug into his back.

"No—stand just where you are, Spider!" Henry Mallon gritted. "I can shoot, too—and I will if you make any move against me. O'Neill," he commanded his reporter, "call the police. Tell them that John Gregg has been murdered—and that I am holding the killer."

Out of the corner of his eye Wentworth could see the open door of the wardrobe, the side drawer of Mallon's desk pulled wide—and he knew, too late, how the managing editor had suddenly gotten the upper hand.

Now that he had it, Mallon meant to keep it. The gun muzzle never moved from Wentworth's spine while O'Neill made the call to headquarters, held steady there for long minutes after the call was finished... fleeting minutes that were bringing the police closer and closer.

To attempt a break would be fatal.

Wentworth knew that; but he waited, matching his peerless nerves against Mallon's... waited, every muscle tense and ready... waited—until he caught the sound of the police sirens, and felt that muzzle yield ever so slightly.

That was the moment! In a flash perfectly coördinated muscles went into action. Flinging himself around and to one side, Wentworth's right arm whipped behind his back and knocked the gun aside just as Mallon's finger pressed the trigger. The burned powder singed Wentworth's coat, but the bullet bored harmlessly into the paneled wall—and before the editor knew what had happened he was looking into the muzzle of his own revolver.

"Downstairs, Mallon," Wentworth rasped. "I need your car and your chauffeur. I am an old friend of yours, and you are instructing your man to take me wherever I wish to go—*understand?*"

Mallon nodded glumly. He was licked, and knew it. Docilely he accompanied Wentworth to the street and gave the chauffeur the required orders. With a firm handshake and a broad smile, Wentworth stepped into the limousine and started uptown— just as the radio cars began to converge on the *Chronicle* building from every direction.

He was safe, Wentworth admitted as he sank back on the soft upholstery. He had danced his way out of what had seemed a dead-end trap—but the damage was done, nevertheless… Damage irreparable.

Now there would be no stopping that devilish edition with its fiendishly retouched photograph. The moment Mallon got back to his desk he would start shouting orders that would make Richard Wentworth a fugitive, a red-handed murderer, definitely identified and hunted as the Spider!

CHAPTER 5
MASTER OF MURDER

THE MOMENT word of that extra reached police headquarters, Wentworth realized, Kirkpatrick's men would start for Sutton Place with a warrant for his arrest. After that the stronghold would be watched night and day. It would be closed to him—as would every other refuge in New York.

Richard Wentworth must disappear—and in a hurry—for no doubt Mallon had already given the alarm and police radios were even now broadcasting a description of his limousine. The danger of being stopped and recognized became greater with every block now. But where could he go?

The car now moving up Broadway, approaching Union Square.

"All right, chauffeur," he called through the speaking tube. "I'm getting out here—at that B.M.T. subway station."

For a moment he thought the driver did not intend to obey. Then the limousine came to a stop, and he was out before the Oriental had a chance to open the door. For a moment their eyes clashed—and Wentworth was certain that he detected a flash of venomous hatred in the suave countenance.

Perhaps the chauffeur had correctly interpreted that little drama in front of the *Chronicle* office. In that case, he probably would rush to the nearest policeman, the moment he was out of sight. However that would make little difference now. In a few moments Wentworth had lost himself in the labyrinthian maze of the Fourteenth Street subway junction and it would have taken scores of policemen to locate him.

Even then, they never would have recognized the man who finally emerged from one of the underground men's room. He was no longer Richard Wentworth, but a quite different-looking

Gordon Powell, a traveling salesman who maintained a small furnished apartment on East Twenty-fifth Street.

There he completed his transition with a change of clothing, a flashy, "up-to-the-minute" outfit that would have amazed the friends who knew Wentworth as a model of good taste. Richard Wentworth disposed of, but sharp eyes and keen ears would be on the lookout for the slightest clue that might reveal his trail. Even to attempt to get in touch with Sutton Place by telephone now would be dangerous.

Wentworth avoided this danger by walking to East Thirty-sixth Street, where Jackson was keeping his vigil in sight of the Warrington home. Quickly Wentworth explained the situation and arranged a rendezvous for the morning.

"We'll have to let Warrington shift for himself now," he decided. "It is more important that you get back to Sutton Place and spell Jenkyns at the garage phone. I want someone there every minute."

From Jackson, Wentworth went to the street where big Mike Fogarty was keeping watch outside the building that housed Kenneth Rockwell's apartment. Fogarty, a trusty private detective who had on many occasions proved himself invaluable to Wentworth, had his heavy bulk propped up against a bar from which he could keep the building in sight.

"Sure is an exciting life I lead," he growled after Wentworth had made himself known. "That feller must be a hermit, and the place must be a morgue. Hasn't been a soul come in or out of it all day. Hell of a life, but you're paying for it." He shrugged and chewed away at the butt of a cigar jammed in the corner of his mouth.

The rest of that night was as quiet as had been Mike Fogarty's day. Patsy DeLott seemed to be lying low, and his gangsters made no further show of violence. But Wentworth knew that this was only the lull before the storm. By eleven-thirty, he was able to buy a copy of the next day's edition of the *Chronicle*—and then the storm broke.

There, on the first page, was the photograph he dreaded, beneath it the screaming headline that branded him as the Spider. But now he and the Withering Death monopolized almost the whole page. Alongside the account of the raid on Patsy DeLott's club was the story of John Gregg's murder—charged squarely against Wentworth. In a desperate effort to keep his Spider identity secret, the *Chronicle* declared that he had murdered the city editor who was about to expose him.

The case was so cleverly built up that no one could help but believe it. With that ghastly picture to back it up and excite the imagination, the city would be clamoring for his head in the morning....

But far more important to Wentworth were the ravages of the Withering Death that were reported in the other columns. Half a dozen customers had been locked in the Parisiana nightclub and held there an hour, to find themselves stricken with the Withering Death when they were released—because the Parisiana proprietor refused to pay the extortion money that had been demanded of him. Four customers had been unable to get out of the brokerage office of Gerald Tyson, when the doors refused to open—and when they finally were released their skins were already beginning to shrivel and darken as the mummy death fastened its grip upon them.

Like the owner of the Parisiana, Tyson admitted that he had been threatened over the telephone, and also exhibited the gruesome hand that he had found on his desk. He had refused to be held up—and his customers had paid for his defiance.

Callous, cold-blooded murder of the most terrifying sort! Wentworth's eyes frosted as they traveled from column to column. The daughter of a banker stricken in her home... The wife of an importer who left to visit her daughter—and came back a ghastly mummy... A well known Broadway gambler who was found, mummified and handless, in his bed....

The list was growing as the Withering Death fastened itself upon the city, and with each case the papers reported the terror was spreading. These victims were the defiant ones who had refused to pay. How many others, Wentworth wondered, were pouring their wealth into Patsy DeLott's pockets?

By morning the toll was even greater.

WHEN MIKE FOGARTY came to the Gordon Powell apartment he brought with him copies of the latest papers—special editions that screamed the news of the mummy horror to a city that already felt the desiccated fingers of an armless hand clutching at its throat. Now the papers had learned that the most expert of the city's doctors and scientists had failed utterly to discover the means by which this ghastly fate was inflicted.

The city's medicos were stumped—and three of them, as well, had vanished on the previous day. Dr. Carter Gregory had gone out to answer a call and had failed to return. Dr. Frank Colbert had been summoned to a consultation with Dr. Menas Hinsey—and both of them had vanished....

What was this, the *Chronicle* wanted to know—the beginning of a campaign to strip the city of its doctors so that it would be utterly helpless against the threat of the Withering Death?

"I know that punk, DeLott," Mike Fogarty growled, as he sat in conference with Wentworth, "and you can't tell me he could pull a thing like this. It's spreading all over the city, scaring hell out of everyone. He could get away with that down in the slums where he lives, but he ain't got the brains for anything as big as this."

Then who—if not DeLott? Henry Mallon, of the *Chronicle!* It was not beyond possibility that it was he who had terrorized John Gregg—he who had managed to murder the city editor in those few minutes when Wentworth was out of the office. Or was it Kenneth Rockwell, as Kirkpatrick had suggested? A case could be built up against the Egyptologist.

"Rockwell!" Fogarty swore fervently. "I'm getting old, Mr. Wentworth—losing my memory. I wanted to tell you about him—tried to get you last night and you were out. Maybe it's nothing—but he did have a visitor a couple hours after I saw you. Dopey Weasel—know him?"

Wentworth nodded, and the face of a thin, mild-mannered man who looked like a school teacher flashed into his mind.

"Well, he came around there about ten o'clock," Fogarty said. "I got close enough to see him jab his thumb on the middle button. That's Rockwell's. The door opened and he went up.

Stayed about twenty minutes and came down alone. Queer sort of guy to be hanging out with Rockwell, ain't he?"

He was.

Wentworth was well acquainted with Dopey Weasel and had often been in the dope joint over which he presided. Dopey Weasel was one of the most astute, the "slickest," characters of the underworld. He might well have established himself as its undisputed overlord were it not for his one outstanding weakness—his inability to resist the lure of the dope he peddled. Periodically his keen brain was fogged and he went into retirement until his bout with the dope was finished. Then for weeks, perhaps even months, he was himself again, free from his terrible curse.

But what possible contact could Dopey Weasel have with Kenneth Rockwell? Into Wentworth's mind flashed Stanley Kirkpatrick's suspicions. Kirk had said that, of course, Rockwell must have a confederate. Could it be possible that Dopey Weasel was the man? Possible that the Weasel had at last mastered his weakness and taken up crime on a grand scale?

Certainly Dopey Weasel had a far better equipment for that role than Patsy DeLott....

DeLott and the Weasel were almost neighbors. Both were at home in the most congested section of New York's slums, and there the trail of the Withering Death seemed to lead. Richard Wentworth would have been helpless trying to follow that trail, once it disappeared in the mazes of the underworld—as helpless as Stanley Kirkpatrick and his most capable men had proved themselves to be time and again.

But for one of their own kind the resorts of gangland held no barriers, and Blinky McQuade had long been accepted as one of their own....

LEAVING FOGARTY to resume his vigil over Kenneth Rockwell, Wentworth taxied downtown to a street corner several blocks east of the Bowery. There he got out and continued his way on foot, through narrow streets that frequently were jammed from side to side with stalled traffic and noisy humanity. Once he left the cab he seemed to be lost in that human rabbit-warren, but his way led directly to a squalid thoroughfare labeled Holian Alley but dubbed "Holy Alley" by its habitues.

Holian Alley ran only a few blocks and came to an end when it merged with equally smelly and ill-favored Pallin Place. It was at the intersection of these two that Wentworth turned into the doorway of a grimy, disreputable-looking building and climbed to its second floor. There a key let him into a barren, shabbily furnished rear room.

The most imposing article of furniture in that room was a massive and ancient bed—and to this he went immediately. Pressing his fingers against its high headboard, he released a panel that opened out to offer a complete make-up table and kit.

This bed was the spot from which Blinky McQuade customarily emerged into the world. Skillfully Wentworth's supple fingers worked on his face, and gradually it changed, became transformed, lost the glow of health and became sickly and neglected looking. Out of that metamorphosis came a slovenly-looking individual with sallow face and weak, pendulous lower lip; an oldish man with gray hair and frowsy face, who

peered out at the world from behind metal-hooded glasses—
Blinky McQuade, former safe-blower and present-day cracks-
man of no mean reputation.

A seedy-looking, grease-stained suit and a sweat-grimed
slouch hat that had lost all vestige of shape—and now Wentworth was ready to step into that part of the world that is
known to few but those who compose it. A part that knew and
accepted Blinky McQuade without question, never suspecting
that Blinky had come into being only so that the Spider might
penetrate to those underworld haunts and rendezvous where
even his deadly guns could not blast a way for him.

Shambling out of Number One Holian Alley with his usual
furtiveness, Blinky shouldered his slovenly way through the
swarming streets until he reached the "hotel" where Dopey
Weasel's guests could obtain a night's lodging for fifteen cents.
The reading-room, in the front of his flop-house, was crowded
with human derelicts, as always, but Blinky paid them no attention. He shuffled up to the desk, mumbled to the clerk, was
looked over carefully and recognized and then passed through
a gate that led to a corridor and a stairway to the rear of the
floor above.

There was no crowd in the big room on the second floor. Even
fewer than usual of the initiates were on hand, and Blinky sensed
at once that something unusual was on foot.

That room was lined with lounges and cots, with settees and
easy-chairs—where those of Dopey's customers who did not
feel they could afford the expense of a private cubbyhole might
enjoy the effects of his wares. Blinky dropped into a chair and

looked around him—and almost at once the Weasel was there at his side, grinning down at him.

"Where in hell you been keeping yourself, Blinky?" the proprietor inquired, genially. "Ain't seen you in ages. Talking about you only the other night and wondering where you were. Come on up front a couple of minutes. I want to talk to you." He winked, and Blinky followed him into the little room that served as a private office.

"How are the fingers, Blinky?" Dopey inquired solicitously, as soon as they were seated. "Still in practice—"

"Good enough for any crib you got in this joint," Blinky grunted.

"I bet," Dopey chuckled, and his eyes sparkled. Wentworth saw that they were clear and bright, altogether free of dope fog. "You come just in time, Blinky. That's why I was talking 'bout you the other day—I need a good man for a job tonight. No nitro artist. I need a man who can open a crib without damaging it—and can put it back the way it was."

"I dunno. When's this job comin' off?" Wentworth pretended to stall. "I gotta have time to case it."

"Tonight," Dopey repeated. "You don't have to worry 'bout casing—that's all been done. This is a sure thing—no slip-up. You'll have good men to go with you and cover you—and I'm cutting you in right on the take. This is something big, Blinky." He leaned close. "You're not the only one. There'll be other parties—and we'll pool the whole pot for the split. You can't lose. I'll fix you up now, and you can stay here till the others come." Dopey settled the matter without waiting for an acceptance.

Grumbling about not being sure, Blinky allowed himself to be led back into the main room and then into one of the little cubbyholes that adjoined it. There Dopey quickly brought him a supply of heroin and then went out to attend to another customer.

As soon as he was gone, Wentworth emptied the drug from the tiny vial container and then stretched out on the cot and pretended to sleep. As he expected, half an hour later the door opened softly and Dopey Weasel peered in. Then the door closed—and the key turned in the lock.

Whether he wanted to or not, Blinky McQuade had enlisted for the Weasel's job—Dopey was taking no chances of a change of heart. As he lay there, Wentworth wondered what that job might be. Something important. More than that, it must be something on a wholesale scale, or Dopey could not have waited until the last moment to secure his man. But where, if at all, would it tie up with the Withering Death?

WENTWORTH GOT no hint of the answer to that question, as the afternoon passed, but he learned quite a bit about the night's program. The walls of these booths were almost paper-thin, and frequently he caught snatches of conversation from one of the others or from the main room.

Gradually he pieced these hints together, and the answer began to take form. Far from being the old safe-cracker who was to work that evening, he was to be only one of a score or more. This was no small, isolated robbery Dopey Weasel was engineering—it was a mass looting, a criminal coup that would rock the city!

"Yeah, I know," he heard the weasel's low voice arguing down an objection. "They change their best rocks around from store to store—all these chain places do that—but we're knocking them *all* off tonight. *All* of them, get that? We're not taking any chances drawing a blank."

A chain of jewelry stores, scattered all over the city, and all of them to be looted simultaneously—that was the answer! That was why Dopey was so glad to welcome another safe-cracker recruit....

That much Wentworth understood—but there was more than he could catch only in snatches. Something about a "surprise"—something about settling things with somebody—something about "wiring" that seemed to be very important. Those references refused to make sense, but Wentworth forgot about them as he speculated on what lay behind the night's deviltry.

Was this merely robbery on a wholesale scale, a daring raid that was planned for the loot it would bring—or was it part of the program of the Withering Death? He was still debating this when evening came and Dopey called him to join the others for a bite to eat. The others—there were sixty or seventy of them, Wentworth saw to his astonishment, and they seemed to keep coming. A regular criminal army!

Very soon he discovered the identity of his own partners. Dutch Heimer, Jim Cleary and a man named Janecki, who would drive. They stayed with him from the moment the Weasel brought them together, and Wentworth saw that there would be no opportunity for him to slip away for a few moments—no chance to get in touch with Kirkpatrick or with Jenkyns.

It was after nine o'clock when they started. Other parties had gone before, and others were still waiting, for it seemed that the Weasel was synchronizing his raids so that they all would occur at practically the same time. A jewelry store on upper Broadway proved to be Wentworth's own destination—the Corum Credit Jewelers, he read the sign as they approached the dark establishment.

There were at least two dozen Corum stores in Manhattan—enough to yield a haul of tremendous proportions!

CLEARY, WHO was an electrician, approached the place alone while the others waited in the car half-way down the block. In a few minutes he was back, grinning—the burglar alarm had been disconnected, the lock picked. Now it was Wentworth's turn. With Heimer close at his elbow, he followed Cleary into the dark store and located the big safe.

That safe would be no easy proposition, but Blinky McQuade knew his trade. In the old days, they said, he had almost lost his sight when a load of nitroglycerine went off prematurely. Since then he had never trusted explosives but had depended entirely on his sensitive fingers—which was the fiction version of the long hours Wentworth had spent under the tutelage of one of the most expert safe-crackers who ever had operated in New York.

He knew his business, and in a little more than fifteen minutes had the safe open. Eagerly his companions ransacked its drawers, emptying the gems into ready bags, stripping it of everything of value. Finished at last, he expected them to be ready to leave. But Dutch Heimer was still busy, now unwrapping a parcel about six inches square he had taken out of the bag he carried.

Out of the wrappings came a black box that looked like an automobile battery—a box with terminals and wires connected to its top. Heimer set it down very gently in an open drawer of the safe.

"Okay, Jim," he husked to Cleary.

"Rig it up—and be sure you don't bungle it. Weasel's more het up about this damn thing than about what we bring back."

Carefully, Cleary worked over the wiring. When he had finished, the safe doors were hooked up to an infernal machine that would be set off the moment they were opened! The next person who opened that safe would be greeted with an explosion planned to blow him to bits!

Janecki was waiting to step on the gas the moment they were back in the car. The job had gone off without a hitch, and now the store gave no indication that it had been burglarized— not even the slightest warning to the unsuspecting victim who would spring that death trap. Robbery was understandable, but this deliberate and unnecessary aftermath of murder was beyond Wentworth's comprehension.

That trap must be sprung before it could accomplish its diabolical purpose—but how?

As the car sped on its way downtown, the prospect of accomplishing it became slimmer and slimmer; and once he was back in Dopey Weasel's establishment, Wentworth might be held there until morning or later.

He must act now. Somehow he must get back there and

dismantle the death trap—must call Kirkpatrick and have the police rush to the other Corum establishments.

Block after block sped past, and there was no chance to make a break. Block after block—until Cleary, rummaging through the bag of jewelry in his lap, brought out a solitaire of extraordinary size.

"Some rock!" he marveled. "Gee, if this is the McCoy… But, hell it can't be—not this size. Whaddaye think, Dutch?"

It was at this moment that Wentworth interrupted in the well-known and accepted surliness of Blinky, "Hey, pull up—I gotta get out."

Janecki, at the wheel, instinctively slowed down. But he asked wonderingly, "What's eatin' you, Blinky? Ain't you comin' in for your cut?"

"Damn right, I'm comin' in for it," Blinky snarled. "Whata you think? But I ain't comin' now. They sprung this job on me so sudden, I didn't have no time to make my arrangements. There's somebody I gotta see."

"Imagine, a dame datin' up with Blinky!" chortled Dutch Heimer. "She must hate herself. Well, go on—you done your part of the job okay. Clear out."

"Never mind the chatter," Blinky said sheepishly. "Just pull up. I got somethin' important to do."

He was aware of their raucous amusement, but paid no attention as he left the car, and sauntered around the corner. But the instant they pulled away, Wentworth went into swift action. Into a parked taxi, he jumped.

"The Corum store—*fast!*"

The driver eyed his unkempt passenger with disfavor. "Say, mister—"

"Get going," Wentworth snapped. "This is life or death!"

And his words had their effect, for the taxi shot away at once.

There was a car parked in front of the Corum store as they approached. The manager, perhaps notified that something was not as it should be, had now come down to investigate. Wentworth leaped from the taxi even before it braked to a stop, started toward the store on a run—but almost the moment his feet hit the pavement there was a tremendous explosion that shook the ground and shattered the Corum show windows!

Out of the store came staggering a man who was barely able to walk—a man who gripped an automatic and cursed luridly as he limped toward the waiting machine.

"They're dead, Slim," he groaned, as the driver sprang out to help him. "Blown to hell! The minute we opened that damned crib—"

For an instant Wentworth was dazed, and then his brain began to function—fast. The machine was under way, pulling away from the curb, but he raced to where his taxi was parked, threw himself into the seat.

"Follow those birds, buddy," he clipped. "There's a sawbuck premium in it for you if you hang onto their tail!"

That ten-spot offer was even more of an attraction than the explosion. The driver leaped to earn it, and as the cab careened after its quarry Wentworth tried vainly to find an answer to that amazing situation. Instead of an innocent victim, another gang of safe-crackers had stepped in to explode the waiting trap—

and that, he now more than suspected, was exactly what Dopey Weasel had planned....

CHAPTER 6
REWARD OF FAILURE

D OWN TO the lower East Side they pursued the other car, south and then east toward the river, into a neighborhood where most of the traffic ceased shortly after business hours. The cabbie hung onto the trail tenaciously, just keeping his quarry in sight, until the car turned into a side street that led to the river.

From the corner they watched it turn again and swing into a driveway beside the dark bulk of a factory.

"Good job, buddy," Wentworth complimented. "This is as far as we go. Here's your sawbuck—and a fin for the meter."

Then he was out on the sidewalk, mingling with the deep shadows as he made his way toward the factory. Apparently the building was abandoned. Its lower windows were closed with metal shutters, and those above were grimy and neglected looking. But tonight it appeared to be doing business. Another car turned into the street and sent him scurrying into a doorway as it passed. Like the one he had followed, it swung into the drive. When he had cautiously picked his way in after it, he found a dozen more parked in the rear of the building.

Most of the cars evidently had just arrived, and from them poured a company of bruised and battered men. Blood and bandages were in evidence everywhere, and some of the men were so badly injured that they had to be helped, even carried, by their groaning, cursing fellows.

The only illumination here in the yard was that which came from the auto lights, and in its fitful splashes it was almost impossible for one man to recognize another. That was all that Wentworth needed. Taking off the hooded glasses that might identify him as Blinky McQuade, he tore a length of cloth from his shirt and bound it around his head—and then fell in line with a number of others who were going in through a doorway on the street level.

Beyond that doorway was a short flight of steps and a dim-lit corridor that ran the length of the building. Evidently once a manufacturing plant of some sort, the factory had been stripped of its machinery. But stacks of packing cases lined the walls and tarpaulin-covered piles of merchandise were heaped on the floor. Wentworth caught a glimpse into some of those packing cases and saw that they were half-filled and had been consigned to firms in all parts of the country. As he had suspected, this abandoned factory was a fence, a hideout and clearing house for stolen goods. Wentworth hung back on the rear of the crowd, watched his chance and darted behind the cases. There was no light, only cramped crouching space, but what he had to do must be done now, quickly. Hurriedly, he pulled from underneath his clothes the cloak and collapsed hat of black, found the pocket kit—swiftly transformed himself into the Spider. A hasty job, but it would have to do—*must* do!

Quickly, silently, he hurried after his former companions, loitering just long enough to allow the last one to pass, yards ahead of him, through a door. Nearly a score of men had by now gathered in this large room at the front of the building. They were shoving forward toward a desk at which sat—Patsy DeLott!

Because they all faced DeLott, it gave Wentworth the only possible chance of entering that room—by taking a half-bending position well in their rear. But he need not have worried. At that minute these men, impassioned, eyes glaring hatred, at thought only for their leader.

DeLott seemed to have lost some of his stature as he sat there regarding the new arrivals with wide eyes. His red face looked pale and haggard, and his eyes shifted uneasily as he met accusing glances on every side. Even his loud voice had lost much of its bellowing bluster, and he squirmed like a man who knows he is trapped.

One after the other they arrived, bruised and crippled, like the flow of casualties from a battle-front. And always the report was the same.

"Somebody give us a double-cross… It was waitin' there for us, an' we walked right into it… Hymie never had a chance; he was blown all to hell… Fine cased job that was—with a bomb waiting for us… I dunno how I got out alive; the whole place was wrecked… You fellers got the same dose we did, eh? There's somethin' damn rotten about this…."

Like Dopey Weasel's outfit, these men had made a concerted raid on all the Corum jewelry stores—and everywhere they had met sudden death the moment the safe doors opened. DeLott's spectacular burglary scheme had been an utter failure—had gone so completely haywire that these men who had lived through it wanted to know why. To their suspicious minds there was only one answer—treachery, a sell-out.

"Thought you said this job was cased, Patsy?" a man whose swollen face was black and blue demanded. "Thought everything was covered?"

"One of these places might have pulled a fast one," another growled, "but how come they were all ready for us?"

"It ain't the Corum outfit," put in Lefty Lomack, a

He leaped at DeLott from behind and wrapped his arm around the big man's neck in a strangling grip!

78

power-hungry gangster who had long been one of DeLott's right-hand men. "They wouldn't bust up their own joints that way. Somebody else had it in for us. Looks like somebody took a crack at Patsy—and we got it smack in the puss."

That found fertile ground in their bitter, rebellious minds.

Patsy DeLott had failed them. One of his enemies had put it over on him, had given him a body blow—and they had been on the receiving end. Patsy was licked, finished. He could no longer be trusted—and, by his own code, there was only one reward for failure.

Grumbling and snarling abuse, they started to close in on him, but DeLott read their intentions. Heaving his big bulk out of the chair, he backed away warily, his threatening gun in hand.

"Stay back!" he warned hoarsely. "Stay away from me, you dirty punks! I'll drill the first—"

That was when Lefty Lomack sprang.

Treacherously he leaped at DeLott from behind, wrapped his arm around the big man's neck and whipped his head back in a strangling grip. Like a pack of wolves the vengeful mobsters closed in—and then froze in their tracks when the empty building reverberated with an eerie, cackling howl... and a twisted black figure dropped into their midst, seemingly from nowhere. The Spider!

STRAIGHT AT Lomack the Spider dived, to seize the fellow by the shoulder and hurl him backward, free of DeLott. And then those deadly automatics were unsheathed, pouring lead into the thieves, driving them back from their prey. The Spider wanted Patsy DeLott alive, not dead.

One against thirty or more, he hovered there, weaving and crouching behind the heavy desk as the thugs recovered from their surprise and turned their guns on him. Those odds were far too great. He could not hope to outshoot all of them....

But Patsy DeLott was not yet through.

The moment he was freed from Lomack's grip he backed toward the wall. From the corner of his eye the Spider watched— saw him reach the wall, saw his left hand grope behind him, feeling for something.

Suddenly there sounded a deep, hollow *boom,* the whole building shook and rattled—and the floor of that room bellied and rose, only to collapse and crash down into the cellar below, carrying most of the gangsters with it. In the nick of time the Spider threw himself backward. The floor was already giving way beneath him as he leaped. But he cleared the gaping hole and sped after DeLott, caught up with the fleeing mob leader just as he reached another corridor.

DeLott turned with a snarl and lashed savagely at the Spider's head with an automatic, but suddenly his arm was imprisoned in a vise-like grip, was twisted backward until he screamed and begged for mercy. The Spider had him down, was on top of him, that hideous face leering down into his own, the black-cloaked body perched on his as if he were some helpless insect in the grip of a deadly tarantula.

Cold sweat stood out on DeLott's face.

His mouth hung open, slobbering with terror.

"I know—I know what you think—but I didn't have anything to do with that picture! So help me God, I didn't, Spider!" he babbled. "I don't know anything about it—"

"Or about these mummy deaths!" the cracked voice mocked.

"Not a thing! I don't know no more than you do about that, Spider—except that they're after me, too. I never know when

I'm gonna get mine. That's the truth, Spider—I can prove it. Let me up from here. Let me take you in back and show you—"

Wentworth allowed him to rise and lead the way to the rear of the deserted building. There, in a room that looked as if it once might have been the factory office, he switched on an electric bulb above a steel door set in one of the brick walls. In the center of that door was a slit with a movable cover, like a prohibition speakeasy peep-hole.

"There it is, Spider," DeLott pointed. "Look and see for yourself. There's the secret of the withered mummies."

His gun covering DeLott, Wentworth approached that door, making sure that the gangster-politician was well out of reach. Stepping up to the slit, he pushed the blind aside and peered through—and then the ceiling seemed to come crashing down on his head! Dazed, half-stunned, he staggered backward—and caught a glimpse of the club that had hit him, now sliding back into its groove in the wall.

Too late he realized that the wily DeLott had guarded the approach to that door with a lever-operated bludgeon that must be connected with a section of the floor. His head rang like a great bell, and his senses dulled as nausea overwhelmed him. Vaguely he knew that he was falling, and subconsciously he tried to scramble back to his feet. But DeLott was upon him in a flash and had wrenched the gun from his hand. Hauling him to his feet, the gangster unlocked the steel door and dragged him to it, started to thrust him into the brightly lit interior.

Wentworth fought desperately, but there seemed to be no strength in his muscles.

DeLott handled him like a child—until suddenly there was a rush of footsteps and something came hurtling through the semi-darkness—something that leaped upon DeLott's back and flailed savagely at his face.

In a moment the mobster was pulled free from Wentworth, was sprawled on the floor with someone at his throat, and Wentworth staggered to his feet. Now the pain in his head was subsiding, his senses once more beginning to function… But that attacker who had saved him from DeLott was getting up from the floor, was cursing the fallen gangster!

Wentworth caught a glimpse of his face, and recognized the hate-twisted features of Dopey Weasel!

"Come on, let's get out of here, Spider," Weasel urged, as he grabbed Wentworth's arm and started to pull him toward the door. "That's DeLott's mob coming—let them take care of the dirty skunk."

WENTWORTH WAS out in the corridor before he managed to break the Weasel's hold and shake him off. Shouting to one another in the darkness, DeLott's gangsters were now combing the building. It might be only a matter of minutes before they found him, but before they arrived Wentworth must return to that room. For two reasons: DeLott—and what he had glimpsed in that steel-doored room.

Back into the brick-walled room Wentworth dashed. But before he could reach DeLott, he heard the man scream fearfully—like a man plunging from a great height to his death. At that moment the light above the steel door winked out, and something came rushing through the darkness.

For a fraction of a second Wentworth caught a half-glimpse of a mummified face as the thing leaped past him. Vainly he tried to grasp it, but the apparition threw him off, knocked him backward—and something flew past his face... something that splashed wetly against the wall behind him.

All that happened within a few seconds, and then he was crouched in the doorway of the room, blazing away at the oncoming thugs revealed by the dim corridor lights. Under that deadly fire, they quickly lost heart. Three or four went down, and the rest turned in panic, to stampede back through their fellows. Instantly Wentworth was back in the room, stabbing through the darkness now with his pocket-flash—looking for DeLott.

The gang-leader was cowering on the floor, trembling and whimpering like a child. All the fight had gone out of him; any thought of resistance or flight. Brokenly he cowered there, dabbing at his face and throat with the sleeves of his coat and the tails of his shirt.

As Wentworth came nearer and bent over him, he saw that the man's face and upper clothing were covered with a reddish liquid that looked like diluted blood. Some of it DeLott had managed to wipe off his face—but where it had been the revealed skin was already wrinkling, turning a horrible mummy-brown.

"Pull yourself together, DeLott!" Wentworth lashed at him. "Try to be a man—if you expect to get out of here alive!"

But DeLott made no attempt to move. He seemed to be stunned, to be utterly paralyzed by what had befallen him.

"It's no use, Spider," he whimpered.

"It's no use—nothing can help me now. I'm going to be like

them—a dried-up mummy! I knew this would happen—I did my best to prepare for it. That's why I have those docs there in the steel room. But it's too late!" His voice rose to a wail. "They can't help me now—nobody can help me!"

When Wentworth tried to prod him to his feet, he whimpered, "Leave me here, Spider... It'll be better if they kill me—"

"I'm not leaving you here," Wentworth clipped, as he reached into DeLott's pocket and took his keys. "You're valuable now, DeLott—lots more valuable than you've ever been in your whole rotten life."

THE STEEL door was still unlocked. Wentworth sprang to it, opened it wide, and then stepped into the vault-like interior. Chained there to the steel walls were three captives. Three men whom he recognized, from their published photographs, as the missing physicians, Carter Gregory, Frank Colbert and Menas Hinsey. Stretched out on the floor between them were two rigid mummies—more of DeLott's men who had succumbed to the Withering Death. Beside them lay the doctors' bags and an array of bottles and surgical equipment.

So that was how Patsy DeLott had tried to save himself! Desperately afraid that he, too, would be stricken by the fatal malady, he had had these physicians kidnaped and imprisoned there to work over the mummies; had held them captive in a mad attempt to force them to find a cure for the Withering Death....

Quickly Wentworth freed them from their chains.

"We have to move fast, gentlemen," he told them. "DeLott's mob may find the courage to charge in here at any moment. I want to get him out before they do. He has been stricken with the Withering Death—just contracted it. If we can get him to a hospital, you will have a chance to watch the ravages of the disease almost from its start."

The medicos agreed with him immediately. Gathering around DeLott, they lifted him with rubber-gloved hands and carried him out into the corridor, while the Spider scouted ahead with ready guns. A few scattered shots greeted him, but the gangsters fled before his charge, and after that they made no trouble. Without further interference Wentworth led the way to the back door and the parking-space in the rear. There he requisitioned one of the cars that had a key in the ignition lock—and watched as its tail-lights disappeared down the street.

Already his fingers were busy stripping off the Spider's trappings and make-up, and in a few minutes it was Blinky McQuade who stepped out of the shadows and turned his footsteps toward Holian Alley.

Much had transpired that night—much that seemed to make very little sense; that seemed only to complicate the mummy death muddle.

What was happening in the underworld? Was this an ordinary gang feud into which he had stepped? Perhaps—but where did those mummified bodies fit into it? Patsy DeLott, it now appeared, had not been using that terrifying doom as a weapon. Instead, he had been cowering beneath it, in mortal fear.

Was that the work of Dopey Weasel?

Was he deliberately undermining his rival gang-leaders so that he could take over their mobs—so that be might weld them into one huge army of crime with himself its dictator and the mummy threat his dread weapon? Was that the secret of the Withering Death? And if it was, where did Kenneth Rockwell, who had received a visit from Dopey Weasel, fit into the crime pattern?

As he plodded through the dark streets, Wentworth knew that he was far from the solution—but how very far he little suspected....

CHAPTER 7
TERROR'S DEATH TRAP

PATSY DeLOTT received every care, every medical advantage that the City of New York could give him. Besides the three eminent physicians whose services he had summarily requisitioned, a dozen of the most renowned specialists visited his bedside in Bellevue Hospital. Everything known to medical science was done for him... but his big body fairly melted away in front of their eyes.

"He seems to be burning up inside," Dr. Gregory marveled as he stared in amazement at the thermometer that had been taken from the suffering man's mouth. "Such a temperature is unheard of—and yet we have given him every known fever remedy."

Sweat stood out on DeLott's face in great drops, ran down his body in rivulets and soaked the sheets and mattress beneath him.

Quickly the brownish color had spread over his skin, until his whole body was like that if an Indian—a very old and weazened

Indian. Leathery skin that was dry and papery, even while the perspiration oozed from it.

The physicians had given him every test and treatment that might possibly stop that inner burning, yet it went right on. In an incredibly short time Patsy DeLott was turning into a mummy.

There were others in that room besides the doctors. Behind the medical men stood Stanley Kirkpatrick and several of his best detectives, watching and listening to every word that came from DeLott's lips. At first the gangster-politician had refused to talk. Convinced that he was doomed, he had resigned himself to his fate and, like his kind, had glared surly defiance when Kirkpatrick endeavored to question him.

But gradually the consuming fire that raged within him melted down his resistance. A mere shadow of himself, his glazed eyes staring up out of cavernous sockets, he lay there like one dead—and then the thin lips that were drawn tight over half-bared teeth began to move.

At first the sounds were unintelligible.

Gradually they began to form words—detached words that made little sense; and then they became more connected, more understandable. DeLott was talking to someone—answering someone on the telephone. He was promising to obey, promising to do anything—was begging for time, pleading abjectly. At times his mind wandered. Then he would get a fresh grip on himself and talk clearly.

"No—no—Spider! I didn't do it!" he protested hoarsely. "I

don't know anything about that picture! I don't know anything, I tell you—I don't know I—"

His voice rose to a thin shriek that had no substance behind it, and Stanley Kirkpatrick moved closer to the bedside. Grimly he listened to that hysterical babble, and each word seemed to knife deep into his heart.

Something had gone out of Kirkpatrick's life the night before when he stepped into the *Chronicle* office and saw John Gregg's body with the Spider's mark stamped on his forehead—and then had been confronted with that damning photograph the paper was about to publish. He had long been almost positive in his conviction that the Spider and Richard Wentworth were one, but to have the actual proof placed in his hands—to realize that Wentworth could have committed such a cold-blooded murder in order to keep his identity a secret—took something vital out of him.

"He came in here with a gun and forced me to call Gregg to the office," Henry Mallon had testified. "Then he forced me into that wardrobe and waited to get the drop on Gregg. I heard him tell Gregg that he was going to take him somewhere after Gregg had changed the first page to eliminate that Spider story—and then I heard Gregg groan. When I managed to get the wardrobe door open, Gregg was sitting there like that and Wentworth was at the window, trying to find a way to escape."

Young Ted O'Neill had added his testimony, but it was of little value—except to damn Wentworth. He could not say what might have gone on in Mallon's office before Wentworth came to his rescue in the corridor. He could not even be certain that

Wentworth's show of surprise on discovering Gregg's body had not been staged for his benefit.

After that atrocious murder and double-barreled identification, Kirkpatrick knew, there remained only to capture Wentworth and convict him—remained only the jury trail with its certain result, and then the execution.

Now, as he stood there staring down at DeLott's wasted body, the commissioner could visualize every detail of that dooming sequence. And as he listened to the dying man's wild raving, he became convinced that there could be no mistake. Driven at last into the open, the Spider was desperate; was willing even to unite forces with such a murdering fiend as the one behind this Withering Death in order to save his own life.

That left no choice but to round him up and clap him in jail at the earliest possible moment. After that, Kirkpatrick knew with taunting certainty, life would be even more empty and futile than it was at this moment. Yet his eyes narrowed and his saturnine features became bleak.

The end was very near for Patsy DeLott. The mere skeleton that was all that remained of his big body hardly moved now. The wild delirium had subsided until his mumbling was hardly audible—and then it was stilled entirely.

Woodenly Stanley Kirkpatrick turned away from the latest victim of the mummy doom, and spoke to the reporters who waited in the doorway.

"I am adding to the five-thousand-dollar reward posted by the *Chronicle*, my own offer of a like amount," he clipped grimly. "That is for the apprehension of the Spider—dead or alive!"

THE WITHERING DEATH

WHEN RICHARD WENTWORTH read that announcement the next morning, he knew exactly how Kirkpatrick felt. His heart went out to his friend—and, at the same time, he realized how utterly alone he now stood.

Again the morning papers were filled with terrifying accounts of the Withering Death, and the roll of mummies grew longer. Five passengers had been trapped in an elevator in the Ashley Apartments when it became stalled between two floors—and when they finally were released, the stamp of doom was already spreading over their bodies.

Six convention delegates playing cards in a room at the Savonia Hotel had sat at the table until the darkening complexion of one of them had startled the others—and then it was too late, for all six of them had been stricken.

Reluctantly the managers of the Ashley and the Savonia admitted that they had refused to heed the demands of the Mummy Hand when it appeared in their offices.

Horror piled on horror, and Wentworth saw clearly the effect this mounting terror was certain to have. To refuse tribute meant doom, swift and inescapable—for the one threatened or his friends and associates. The Withering Death struck with utter ruthlessness—and the police were able to do nothing to check it. In the face of that certain doom, defiance was worse than foolish. Rather than jeopardize the lives of innocent people, as well as their own, most men would pay—and keep silent.

Millions of dollars must be flowing into the bloody hands of the callous fiend. But who could that fiend be?

Again Wentworth went over the list of possibilities—and had

91

PETER HENNESSEY   KENNETH ROCKWELL   MIKE FOGARTY

to admit that the name of Kenneth Rockwell would not down. Who was that creature, that mummy-faced apparition, who had almost bathed him with the deadly mummy poison last night in the abandoned factory? Could that have been Kenneth Rockwell, working hand in hand with Dopey Weasel?

It was quite possible that Weasel had brought the young Egyptologist to the factory with him. That might have been the reason the Weasel was so anxious to get the Spider out into the corridor—so that Rockwell would have a free hand to douse Patsy DeLott with the fatal mixture.

Certainly, Wentworth decided, it was time he had a talk with Kenneth Rockwell.

In the guise of Gordon Powell he went to the Consolidated Museum, but the man was not there and had given no indication when he might be expected. Nor was he at home. Wentworth looked in vain for Mike Fogarty. He, also, had disappeared, no doubt on Rockwell's trail.

WARRINGTON   JUDITH MALLON   CHEN-AH-LO

It wasn't until late afternoon that Wentworth caught up with them, through the unlisted phone behind one of the Sutton Place garages. Mike Fogarty had called; had left a number.

"I been trailing this bird all over town today," the detective growled when Wentworth called him, "but he's gone to roost at last. He's not staying at the old place anymore—got another apartment up here on West Seventy-second Street. Phony name in the bell—but it's him all right."

Wentworth jotted down the number, and twenty minutes later he stepped out of the elevator on the ninth floor of a fashionable apartment house. Something about that building struck a reminiscent chord in his mind, but he dismissed it as he approached the apartment Fogarty had spotted.

Twice he pushed the button, while he waited close—pressed against the doors. But there was no response. Fogarty had been certain that Rockwell was in there, but evidently he was not answering the bell. Tensely Wentworth listened—and was almost certain he heard the creak of a board in the hallway beyond the door. Then silence....

For more than five minutes he waited.

Then, cautiously, his adjustable skeleton key slipped into the spring lock. Silently it turned as he gripped the knob—and then pushed the door wide and quickly stepped back from the jamb.

THE DOOR opened into a small foyer, and beyond that was a living-room. For a moment the archway between them was empty, and then Kenneth Rockwell stood silhouetted in it, his face blanched and his eyes wide. His lips moved, stammered inarticulately.

Wentworth had stepped into the foyer and closed the door. "All right, Rockwell—nothing to worry about," he reassured.

"Oh, it's you—Wentworth!" Rockwell gasped his relief. "Man, I *am* glad to see you! I've wanted to get hold of you all afternoon but didn't know how to reach you. I knew you wouldn't be home—after what I saw in the papers. I've been sitting here wondering what to do—"

"Why the change of apartment—and the alias downstairs?" Wentworth asked as he made a quick inventory of the place.

"Because I have been followed—spied upon." Rockwell's eyes clouded and his mouth twitched nervously. "Men have been watching my apartment, and they have been making inquiries of Mrs. Platt, my landlady. She said they looked like detectives, but I'm not taking any chances. They may belong to the same murdering gang who murdered Sue and are now terrorizing the whole city... I haven't given up hope of avenging her, Wentworth." He leaned forward in his chair and spoke earnestly. "Since the night she died, I have been racking my brain for a clue to the monster who did that ghastly thing to her—*and I think I know who he is!* That's why I wanted to see you. He is quite firmly entrenched—and I don't know just what to do."

"You know him?" Wentworth's blood raced. "Who is he?"

"George Bradley—the head of the Sedgwick Rest Home, the private sanitarium where the city has been segregating the Withering Death victims," was the answer. "He has more of them up there than anyone knows—thirty or forty I heard just a little while ago—and I am convinced that he has been feeding them into the place deliberately, so that he can get complete control of them.

"You want to know why I suspect him, of course. For several reasons. In the first place, he was formerly one of Sue Warrington's suitors. He supposed that he had everything his own way, until I came along—and he wasn't a graceful loser, to say the least. I know that he hates me, and I suspect he hated Sue—perhaps even enough to murder her."

Rockwell frowned. "I became suspicious when the city picked his sanitarium as an isolation place. It took influence to get that for him—influence that he must have had some good reason for exerting. But, most important of all, one of the nurses in his place is a good friend of mine—Margaret Allen. I have been keeping in touch with her—and the things she has reported have more than confirmed my suspicions. Read this," and he unfolded a sheet of notepaper he took from his pocket.

It was a brief note, in feminine handwriting.

"Dear Kenneth," Wentworth read, "I am smuggling this out to you because I do not know how much I will be able to say over the phone. Things are terrible here. You ought to be here—or get somebody in to see what is going on. If I could tell the police what I know, but I am helpless. Can't you do something?—Margaret."

"I spoke to her a little while ago," Rockwell added, "and she was excited. She thinks there is something planned for tonight, but I didn't know what to do."

"Can she get us inside?" Wentworth planned swiftly.

"I don't know, but I can find out."

Rockwell reached for the phone and dialed a number, asked for Margaret Allen and talked cryptically for several minutes. "Eight-thirty," he nodded to Wentworth as he put down the receiver. "She will be there to meet us when we arrive."

Eight-thirty—that was still more than two hours. Wentworth sat back and speculated what awaited them at the Sedgwick Rest Home—and also speculated on the nervous young man who watched him from across the living-room. Kenneth Rockwell seemed sincere. His manner was earnest, anxious—and yet there was a tensity about him that betrayed an excitement he did his best to conceal.

Was it the prospect of coming to grips with George Bradley, the prospect of avenging Sue's death, which caused that excitement? Wentworth wondered, and back into his mind flashed Stanley Kirkpatrick's suspicions.

"How did Austin Warrington like this chap Bradley?" he suddenly ventured a question that came into his mind. "Did he favor him?"

"No," Rockwell shook his head; "but that isn't surprising. He didn't favor anyone who seemed to be making progress with Sue."

"Yourself included?"

"That's no secret," Rockwell shrugged. "Mr. Warrington was passionately fond of Sue, and for that reason he had little use for anyone who threatened to take her away from him. Before I came along, he had managed to break up every one of her friendships that threatened to develop into a serious romance. He tried the same tactics with me, but they did not work. After that he put the best face he could on it, but I knew that he had no great regard for me...."

His voice trailed off abstractedly and he stared blankly into space, evidently revisioning his contacts with Austin Warrington—until suddenly Wentworth's voice cut in on his meditation.

"I heard that you had a visitor the other day, Rockwell—an underworld character they call Dopey Weasel," Wentworth plumped at him. "What did he want with you?"

Startled, Rockwell's eyes blinked in amazement.

A question seemed to hover on his lips. Then he thought better of it.

"He came to ask a lot of questions about Sue," he answered uncertainly. "He was on the trail of that five thousand dollars reward the *Chronicle* offered for your capture."

Which would have been a perfectly plausible explanation, if Wentworth had had any confidence in Rockwell. But now he was certain that the young fellow was concealing something—that he was deliberately playing a most unusual part, and striving desperately to carry it off successfully.

CLOSELY HE watched his companion as a taxicab sped them northward to the Bronx. His keen eyes noted Rockwell's mounting excitement when they drew nearer to the Sedgwick Rest Home. Wentworth followed his restless gaze out of the window, noted the sparse traffic they passed—and then was suddenly aware that the number of cars going past them had increased heavily... a veritable procession.

Peering more closely, he caught a glimpse into the rear of a sedan that passed them beneath an arc-light—and was almost certain that a hideous mummy face had leered out at him before it was yanked back from the window!

Had Rockwell seen that, too? Wentworth swiveled around, but the young fellow's face told him nothing. His eyes were staring straight ahead, his lips clenched into a straight line. The Sedgwick Rest Home was just ahead.

Night had already fallen before they reached it, but they dismissed the cab a block away and went the rest of the distance on foot. A great, gloomy-looking building of weather-darkened stone, the sanitarium was set back from the street some fifty yards and was surrounded by low trees and shrubbery. It was unhealthy looking, a fitting place in which to isolate a plague, but there was something otherwise odd about it….

Lights burned in the three stories of windows, and yet the place had a peculiar air of desertion. The front door was tightly closed, the lower windows shade-drawn, and there was no sign of anyone about.

"Where is your nurse?" Wentworth asked as they stood at the end of the path leading to the building.

"I don't know," Rockwell's voice came in a whisper. "She is supposed to be waiting here. Perhaps if we go up nearer to the building…" Suddenly his voice faltered and stopped. His eyes widened and stared as if a ghost had risen.

Wentworth, too, had heard that muffled scream. His eyes had also flashed to the windows of the sanitarium. There, on the first floor, a shade had been pulled aside and then yanked from its roller. For an instant the slim figure of a nurse was outlined in the lighted window—a young woman who was struggling frantically to pound her fists through the pane.

Before she could succeed, she was caught from behind, was seized in the arms of a horrible-looking creature with the ghastly face of a mummy! Another of those fearful near-corpses reared up beside her—and at that moment the lights in the room snapped out.

The mummies were loose, had seized control of the sanitarium! Driven insane by the shriveling death that was eating at their vitals, they must have gone berserk and overcome the attendants!

Wentworth sped along the path and leaped up the short flight of steps. The front door would be locked, but he grasped the handle—and at his touch the door flew open. Before he could recover his balance he pitched half-way across the hallway—and then three of those mummy creatures were upon him. Fists lashed out at him, hands seized him and dragged him down, and those horrible gargoyle faces glared at him hideously.

Desperately he strove to defend himself, strove to tear loose from the grip of those entwining arms—and as he fought something clamored for recognition in his brain.

Something about this was all wrong....

And then he knew what it was! Those mummy creatures had the emaciated faces of skeletons, but that fist which was swinging at his head—that arm he had just tugged away from around his throat—was *thick, solid....*

That realization gave him fresh strength. Fighting halfway clear of his attackers for an instant, he managed to draw one of his guns—only to have it knocked out of his hand. But at the same moment his fist smashed into one of those bony faces and sent the creature staggering backward. Again his fist lashed out at a second attacker, just as the third grabbed him around the legs and bore him down. They were on him in an instant, swarming over him, suffocating him—until suddenly relief came from an unexpected quarter.

"Get out, you fools!" a voice snarled from somewhere in the rear of the building. "There's no time—"

Wentworth did not hear the rest of it. Suddenly his attackers lost all interest in him. Pell-mell they bolted for the rear and dived through an open doorway at the back of the hallway....

NOT UNTIL then did he have a chance to look around him, and what he saw chilled his blood. The nurse he had glimpsed at the window lay in the doorway of what apparently was the reception room, a pool of blood widening on the floor beneath her head. At the foot of the stairs lay a white-uniformed interne, blood from his smashed skull dying his freshly starched coat a deep crimson.

The place was a shambles, fairly littered with the bodies of nurses and attendants! Getting shakily to his feet, Wentworth recovered his automatic and catfooted through that house of death. The door at the rear of the hallway opened into a corridor that led past the offices, now deserted except for still figures that sprawled on the floor—past one cubicle where a white-haired doctor was struggling vainly to drag himself up to his knees beside his desk.

Instantly Wentworth was at his side.

"What is it?" he barked as he raised the wounded man. "What happened? Where is Bradley?"

"I am Bradley," the old man groaned, "and I hardly know what happened—it came so fast. They seemed to be all over the place at once, killing my staff and taking the patients—"

This was Bradley? But that didn't make sense, a man this age a suitor of Sue Warrington's....

"Where is Nurse Allen—Margaret Allen?" Wentworth tried again.

But the physician shook his head in weak bewilderment; he knew no Nurse Allen. Kenneth Rockwell? That name seemed no more familiar. Bradley evinced no sign of recognition. Wentworth had helped him into an easy-chair, was working over him, trying to keep him from losing consciousness, but the old man was pretty far gone. Valiantly he strove to hold on long enough to say something.

"The mummy patients," he managed weakly. "They took them all—took them in cars—turn them loose on the city—"

The uncertain quaver of his voice was suddenly inundated by a mighty blast of sound as the whole building shook and rocked like a cockle-shell in a hurricane. Instantly the lights went out and the entire structure seemed to be coming down around their ears. Blast after blast followed the first, and echoing each new concussion came the crash and rumble of falling ceilings and walls, of crumbling floors and furniture that danced like dice in a gaming cup.

Wentworth was thrown to the floor with the first blast; felt it cracking and sagging beneath him. He felt himself sliding in the darkness—and then he brought up in the well of Bradley's big desk. What happened after that he hardly knew. All the world seemed to be rending apart with a terrific crashing and grinding. The air was thick with powdered dust that choked him when he tried to catch his breath.

Like a rocket his strange desk shelter shot downward into space, then caromed and bounced crazily, splintered and threatened to break into pieces as he clung to it desperately. Wreckage rained down on top of it, half-buried it, but its sturdy oak top withstood the bombardment and shed the tumbling, crashing missiles.

The sanitarium had been dynamited—dynamited in half a dozen places so that its total destruction was assured. That was what that snarling-voiced warning had meant. The mummy-faced men had fled just in time to escape the building's doom.

Bitterly Wentworth realized that he had stepped into a death-trap; that he had been led into it cunningly by Kenneth Rockwell. Rockwell had played his part well, had succeeded perfectly—even though he probably never would be able to claim the double reward for the battered and broken body of the Spider....

CHAPTER 8
RAID OF THE DOOMED

RESTLESSLY NITA VAN SLOAN paced up and down the Sutton Place living-room and eyed the tastefully decorated walls as if they were the narrow confines of a cell.

That was what the place had become—a prison in which she was confined while Dick was out there somewhere in the city, his life in constant danger from hundreds of reward-hungry thieves and from the very police he tried so hard to aid.

It was bad enough to know of his peril, but if she could *do* something, share the danger with him, the suspense would not be so bad. Instead, she was cooped up here in that stronghold which had let its bars down to the police—was forced to watch Kirkpatrick's men prowl through the place searching for Dick, forced to answer their tiresome and futile questions.

Danger for Dick was nothing new to her. It seemed that the Damoclean sword constantly hung perilously over his head—and yet this was the worst jeopardy in which he had ever been placed. Angrily her eyes turned to the edition of the *Chronicle* that had outlawed him, and then to Kirkpatrick's reward offer.

Stanley should have known better than to believe such utter lies, but he seemed beside himself, a man who had lost all sense of balance. That was the result of this Withering Death, of course, but he should have realized that Dick was doing his utmost, staking his very life, in an effort to uncover and defeat that grisly menace.

If only there were some way in which she could help—but she had gone over that ground hundreds of times. There seemed to be no slightest lead for her to follow, nothing to do but sit there and wait interminably, constantly hoping to hear the tinkle of the telephone and yet fearful each time she lifted the receiver to her ear....

Darkness had settled over the city. It seemed to crowd in

against the wide windows, to hem her in more completely—
until she could stand the confinement no longer. She must get
out, at least for a little while; must walk and breathe the night
air. Perhaps that would calm her nerves and make the endless
waiting more endurable.

"I am going out for a little while, Ram Singh," she decided.
"I want to pick up some things at the drugstore."

RAM SINGH'S dark eyes widened with surprise. He seemed
on the point of objecting, and then thought better of it.

"You will want the car, *missie sahib*," he suggested, and started
for the door.

But Nita stopped him.

"No, I want to walk, Ram Singh," she declined. "It will be
only a few blocks, not worth while taking the car—and you need
not come with me. I shall be back in fifteen or twenty minutes."

His bearded face was filled with foreboding as she left, and
Nita knew that he would trail her at a discreet distance. That was
the responsibility Dick had laid upon him, and to Ram Singh an
order from Richard Wentworth was a thing sacred, a mandate
to be obeyed under any circumstances. But at least she would
momentarily be able to shake off that feeling of confinement
that was fraying her nerves.

Nobody attempted to stop her when she left the grounds by a
side-street entrance. On the corner she spotted one of Kirkpatrick's plainclothesmen, felt his eyes upon her. But he made no
attempt to follow her. Two or three small drugstores she passed,
until she reached a large corner establishment that was part of
the widespread Phelan chain.

There she made her purchases, and then hesitated in front of a row of telephone booths. All day there had been no word from Dr. Rogers. Perhaps he had been in touch with Dick— perhaps even now had news. Impulsively she stepped into one of the booths and dialed the physician's number, heard the buzz of the signal come over the wire....

AS SHE had expected, Ram Singh had not been long in following her from Sutton Place. His dark figure blending with the shadows, the bearded Sikh kept his distance but never let her get out of his sight. To the door of the drugstore he followed her and then took up his vigil on the outside, at a point from which he could follow her movements.

From the counter he saw her step into the telephone booth— and then his vigilant eyes noticed something else.

A sedan had drawn up at the curb in front of the store, and three men were getting out while a fourth remained at the wheel. Two of them were ordinary in appearance—but the third was a ghastly-looking thing that looked as if it had just stepped from the grave!

Swiftly the trio moved. One of them separated from the others and went to the side entrance of the store. The other grasped that hideous apparition by the arm and led it to the main entrance, pushed the door open and shoved the horrid graveling inside, then drew the door closed and planted himself outside of it with drawn guns!

From where he stood, Ram Singh could see that weird-looking mummy hobble into the store, could see that he was holding what seemed to be a length of hose in his bony hand—a hose from which a pinkish vapor was billowing; a vapor that hung in heavy clouds and partly enveloped the customers at the soda fountain.

Instantly that store became a frenzied madhouse, a bedlam of shrieking women and frightened men who sprang away from that fearful monstrosity who glared at them with glassy eyes and drooled meaningless sounds from his horrible, lipless mouth....

In the telephone booth, Nita frowned as she listened to the continued buzz on the other end of the line. That meant no answer; no use waiting any longer. Taking the receiver from her ear, she started to put it back on the hook—and stopped short when that wild burst of screaming broke loose just outside the booth door.

Terrified shrieks—and then the creature that had caused the panic was passing the booth windows. An appalling specter that wore the loose-hanging clothes of a man over the knobby bones of a skeleton! An almost fleshless creature that walked like an automaton, squirting something from a hose that was attached to a metal cylinder strapped at its waist!

Nita felt a cold, clammy trickle snaking down her spine as she stared at that frightful death's-head. That pinkish vapor— instinctively she knew what it was. *The breath of death!* The secret of the mummy doom that the city's foremost scientists were striving in vain to discover. If she could get hold of that cylinder, could wrest it from the creature's grip....

Without thought of consequences, she started to open the booth door—and then she caught sight of Ram Singh. He was just outside the door of the store, was battling with a burly thug.

The almost fleshless creature walked like an
automaton, squirting something from a hose!

But when he realized her intention, he tore free for a moment and wildly motioned to her to keep the booth closed.

That warning almost cost the Sikh his life. Savagely the snarling thug swung at his head with an automatic, and only Ram Singh's tightly wound turban saved him. He staggered back

under the impact of the blow, and then his long, razor-sharp knife snaked out and found its mark.

The thug screamed as the sharp point sank deep into his throat, and then, before his body had slumped to the street, the blade was clear. The weapon reversed and its haft shattered the door window. Swiftly Ram Singh unfastened the end of his turban and wound its folds around his face and neck—but before he could leap into the store and go to Nita's rescue another thug sprang upon his back and hammered at him viciously with a blackjack.

Nita saw the faithful Sikh go down, but his warning had brought her to a realization of her danger. To step out into that poisonous vapor would mean a horrible death. Tight-lipped, she crouched in the booth and drew back as far as possible from the door.

THE PINKISH vapor had almost evaporated when the police arrived, and their clubs, smashing out the door windows, let in a current of air to dissipate what remained. Quickly one of the officers caught the vacant-eyed mummy and tore the hose nozzle out of his bony grip.

"Take that thing off his belt—and be careful of it," the lieutenant in charge ordered.

The policeman was careful. He unbuckled the cylinder, tugged at the strap that held it—and was flung back across the store as the bottom of the metal container exploded and was blown into fragments.

The ghastly mummy was blown into eternity with him—and

with them went the secret of the Withering Death Nita had hoped to secure....

That sudden tragedy added to the wild panic in the store, but the lieutenant had his men lined up, barring both doors as effectively as the gangsters' guns had done before them. Already those luckless victims were beginning to show the effects of the doom that was upon them—their skin ominously darkening where the poisonous vapor had touched it. Carefully the police herded them to one side of the store and kept them there, to wait for the ambulances that would remove them to a hospital.

Not until then did Nita dare emerge from her telephone booth refuge and race for the door.

"I'm all right. I was in a booth—it didn't touch me!" she gasped as the police tried to stop her. Then her eyes widened in surprise.

Ram Singh was just returning to consciousness. Propped up on the sidewalk where he had fallen, he stared down blankly at the handcuffs that encircled his wrists.

"What is that for?" Nita demanded indignantly. "He had nothing to do with this outrage—except to battle with the thugs who staged it. He was trying to break into the store to save me."

"That's what you say, lady," the steely-eyed lieutenant sneered, "but we have witnesses who don't agree with you. Maybe you can explain this gun he was holding in his hand when we found him. A police positive—a stolen department gun. He's under arrest, and maybe I ought to take you in, too."

Nita was still protesting and arguing futilely when another police car sirened up to the curb and Stanley Kirkpatrick hopped out. Swiftly he flung his questions, and in a few minutes he knew what had happened. Grimly he looked down at the torn body of the slain patrolman, and then caught sight of Ram Singh.

"I'm so glad you came, Stanley," Nita approached him confidently. "These men of yours insist on thinking that Ram Singh had something to do with this murderous raid. He was waiting for me outside the store and tried to fight his way in when he saw what had happened—"

"You were *in there?*" Kirkpatrick was incredulous.

"In a phone booth," Nita explained—and her hopes sank as she saw the commissioner's face harden.

"I don't like to think that you had anything to do with a horrible thing like this, Nita," he said coldly, "but it is rather significant that you, and you alone, out of the seventeen customers and clerks in that store, escaped the doom that was sprayed on the rest of them. I should like to feel that it was a coincidence, your being here. But with you in the phone booth and Ram Singh standing guard outside the store with a revolver, I cannot ignore the obvious implication. Ram Singh is under arrest—and I may have to send for you, also."

The man was mad! He had practically insinuated that she had been in that booth to direct the outrage! Nita's anger rose white-hot—and then cooled when she glanced at that huddled group of terror-stricken victims. Already the dread plague was spreading through their blood like wildfire, stamping them with the unmistakable sear skin of the doomed!

Kirkpatrick was not himself. He was almost insane with worry, and well he might be. For as she listened to the reports from newly arrived officers, Nita learned that dozens of stores of the Phelan chain had been similarly attacked that evening.

"There must be close to five hundred people come down with the plague tonight," an inspector reported to Kirkpatrick. "It seems as if every Phelan store in Manhattan got the same dose."

"This is the worst yet," the harassed commissioner groaned. "I knew that the Phelan people had been threatened. But this— after *this* demonstration there isn't a store in the city will dare refuse to come across with whatever the devils demand."

Hundreds of innocent people stricken with a horrible death in order to stage a terrifying demonstration of ruthless power! Nita's blood fairly boiled as she watched those hysterical victims writhing in physical and mental agony; watched them being taken away in ambulances to the hospitals where nothing but ghastly death awaited them.

But what could she do? Now she had been stripped of even Ram Singh's assistance. Yet, as she walked despondently back to Sutton Place, she told herself that there must be some way....

THERE WAS no hope of ever getting out of that deadly trap. Wentworth knew he was doomed, but because it was not in him to give up even in the face of certain defeat, he started to battle the moment the desk that covered him no longer rattled under the barrage of falling wreckage. Cautiously he started to pick his way out from his close-quartered place of refuge, and almost instantly was fairly smothered by the debris that rushed in upon him. To touch one of those crazily crisscrossed beams, to attempt to move a chunk of precariously balanced plaster, meant to bring down on his head an avalanche of smaller wreckage.

Yet Wentworth fought his way upward. Like a mole he tunneled through that loose, treacherous rubble. A dozen times he was almost brained by tumbling fragments; as often it seemed that he must suffocate from the silt-like powder that engulfed him. Struggling prodigiously, battling endlessly in the stygian darkness—and then suddenly there was light. Terrifying light! The ruddy glow of forking flames! The wreckage was on fire!

That dread knowledge drove him to superhuman efforts. Upward... upward... until he was almost clear of the crazy rubbish heap under which he had been buried. Almost clear... and then something slipped. A beam gave way beneath him and undermined a dozen more. The wreckage rumbled and heaved like a volcano. Wentworth slipped back, was buffeted helplessly—and when the movement had quieted he was helplessly trapped beneath a great beam that held him prisoner from the waist down.

After that he battled frenziedly, battled with blind hopelessness, knowing that he would never be able to free himself in time to cheat the on-marching flames. Their cackle was growing louder as the fire spread; was right alongside of him, snapping and crackling at his ear... and now a voice spoke through it.

"Take it easy now," Mike Fogarty warned. "I'm a pretty heavy bird for this Liza on the ice-cake act—but if I can just get this beam lifted I'll have you free."

Mike Fogarty! Wentworth had forgotten all about him—had forgotten that he had instructed the detective to wait outside Kenneth Rockwell's apartment house and continue his vigil until Wentworth came out and relieved him. Following his instructions to the letter, Fogarty had trailed them to the sanitarium.

In that moment Mike Fogarty looked like a delivering angel as his dirty, dust-covered figure loomed above Wentworth. His big hands grasped the imprisoning beam, his powerful shoulders strained—and Wentworth was *free!* Fogarty dragged him clear of the wreckage and helped him to firmer footing, from where they could climb out over a section of the fallen wall.

"What became of Rockwell—did he follow me into the sanitarium?" Wentworth asked as soon as they were clear.

"Like hell he did!" Fogarty growled contemptuously. "He was hiding behind a clump of bushes, watching the place, the last I saw of him. I was keeping an eye on him—until the whole works blew up."

He led the way back to the spot where Rockwell had been crouching, but the other man was gone, and they saw no sign of him in the crowd that was now gathering to gape at the conflagration.

Grim-faced, Wentworth turned away and looked for a taxi to take them back to Manhattan. Kenneth Rockwell no doubt thought that he was dead—that the devilish trap, into which he had baited Richard Wentworth, had spelled his doom. But there was a startling surprise coming to that young gentleman as soon as the cab reached West Seventy-second Street....

THIS TIME Wentworth did not ring the apartment buzzer. For a few minutes he and Fogarty stood outside Rockwell's door, listening but hearing nothing. Then the skeleton key did its work and they stepped into the foyer, their guns ready. But the apartment was empty—seemingly just as it had been a few hours before. Apparently Rockwell had not returned to it.

Carefully Wentworth searched the desk, closets, bureau— and there he found something that prickled his scalp. In the top drawer were four severed and warning-stamped mummy hands! And beside them was a compact electric-battery branding outfit with the iron a duplicate of the Spider's seal! The iron that had branded a raw, crimson spider on the forehead of John Gregg!

Wentworth ransacked every corner of the bureau after that startling discovery—and again he was significantly rewarded. Under the paper lining in the bottom of that top drawer, he found a legal-size envelope that contained a marriage license— filled out with the names of Kenneth Rockwell and Judith Mallon....

Judith Mallon, the daughter of wealthy Henry Mallon, of the *Chronicle!* Astounded, Wentworth stared down at that red-sealed document—and realized that he was looking at what might have been Sue Warrington's death warrant. If Rockwell had wanted to marry Judith Mallon, but had been bound by his engagement to Sue Warrington....

There was the motive Kirkpatrick needed to pin the Warrington girl's murder on young Rockwell!

Wentworth was still holding that sinisterly eloquent license in his hand, when suddenly his every nerve tingled. He had caught a sound, the creak of a board, out in the living-room!

Fogarty had heard it, too. With surprising speed, for a man of his weight, he leaped for the connecting door, was through it a split-second after Wentworth. The room was empty, they saw at a glance—but the window was open. Wentworth was certain that he had heard the metallic scrape of footsteps on the fire-escape beyond. Straight across the living-room he dived, to fling himself out onto the fire-escape landing—just as a black-caped figure, barely distinguishable in the gloom, stepped into the window directly above.

That much Wentworth saw in a flash, then he turned his gaze downward, and understood the meaning of the footsteps he had heard. The lower ladders and landings were alive with climbing figures—swarming with policemen who had already reached the floor below!

Nonplused, he whirled back into the room to meet Fogarty's questioning eyes—just as a door which had been open against the wall swung slowly outward... to spill the staring-eyed corpse of a man face-down on the floor!

Wentworth had caught a glimpse of that down-swinging face, and even before he stooped beside the sprawled body he knew the dead man's identity.

He was Henry Mallon! Henry Mallon, with his torso slit wide open from stomach to throat-and with the brand of the Spider burned deep into his forehead!

CHAPTER 9
FOR ALL TO SEE

WHO HAD been that figure in the black robe who left Mallon's corpse in the apartment before fleeing up the fire-escape? Had it been Rockwell? Had the young Egyptologist been waiting there for them, securely hidden until they arrived? Had he also deliberately brought the police to trap them there? But, if that were so, why would he leave that evidence against himself in the bureau drawer where the searching police would be sure to find it?

Questions without answers—contradictory questions that made no sense—whirled through Richard Wentworth's mind as he and Fogarty sought a way of escape. The fire-escape was cut off, and now they could hear stealthy footsteps outside in the corridor. They seemed hopelessly trapped—but again Wentworth sensed something somehow familiar about this building.

Running to a window, he looked out, scanned the building across the way carefully—and then he had it! That building belonged to Peter Hennessey, and young Hennessey's penthouse was on the roof!

In that penthouse they might find refuge, but how to reach it? Wentworth's brain whirled, planned with lightning speed.

"Come and give me a hand with that corpse, Mike," he whipped to Fogarty. "Out there in the hall with him. We've got to get through that doorway and into the corridor. It's our only chance to reach the roof—and Mallon will have to help us do it."

Quickly he sketched his plan, and Fogarty nodded understanding. He sprang to do his part....

A few moments later Wentworth stepped to the hall door and grasped the knob, twisted it cautiously several times, then waited. A moment more... and now he turned the latch and swung the door inward, flattening himself behind it.

The instant the door opened an automatic roared and a

leaden slug spat out into the hallway. Immediately that shot was answered by a scattered fusillade from the corridor—a fusillade that blazed through the doorway and riddled a dark, barely distinguishable figure now crouching at the rear of the foyer. Half a dozen bullets—then the figure tottered uncertainly, and crashed forward on its face.

Silence settled briefly over the foyer.

It was broken as a uniformed lieutenant and two detectives rushed through the doorway and padded up to that silent figure. One of the plain-clothes men bent over, turned the dead man's head—then gasped in astonishment.

"Hell's bells—that's Henry Mallon!" he gulped in sudden fear that they had committed a terrible blunder. "How in hell—"

But before he got any farther, disaster overwhelmed him. Out of nowhere a big hand closed around his neck and yanked him off his feet, slammed his head with stunning force against the skull of his partner. At the same instant, the lieutenant pitched head over heels and slid into the dark living-room on his face— as the foyer light snapped off and the door clicked shut.

"Stairs—at the end of the corridor!" Wentworth panted as he closed the door and streaked for the rear of the building.

Only two flights to the roof, and luck still seemed to be with them. There was no sign of the police, who evidently had gone no higher than Rockwell's floor. Now Wentworth was on familiar ground. The penthouse was dark, but he quickly located the door and his skeleton key made short work of the lock. He was equally at home on the inside—which was the reason he had come to the penthouse.

Behind the big stone fireplace Peter Hennessey had had the carpenters leave a closet-like recess to which access could be obtained by a panel cleverly concealed in the woodwork. For Hennessey the "hidden room" was a plaything, a gadget he used to play tricks on his friends—but now it promised salvation for Wentworth and Fogarty.

"You'd better go in first, Mike—you'll just about be able to fit," Wentworth chuckled when the panel glided open noiselessly. "It's going to be a tight squeeze for the two of us."

Fogarty backed into the opening, and Wentworth followed. Almost soundlessly the panel clicked back into place, and for long minutes there was no sound but the puffing of Fogarty's asthmatic breath. Then Wentworth felt the big man stiffen, felt him recoil from something in the darkness.

"You said 'two of us,'" Fogarty whispered, "but we've got company in this sardine can. There's two more here, Wentworth—a couple of those mummies, they feel like."

Wentworth flashed on his light and turned it to the back of the cubbyhole, where its beam fell on two leering skeleton heads—two gaunt mummies that were leaning against the wall. A man and a woman who grinned obscenely, as if they hugely appreciated the macabre joke... Two mummies with severed hands!

WHAT WAS the meaning of this discovery? Was this a hideout where the mummy victims were held until they could be disposed of? Was Hennessey tied up with the Withering Death? Was he, perhaps, the Withering Death himself? That seemed incredible. Wentworth knew that the young socialite's means were almost unlimited. Yet other rich men had taken to crime to augment their fortunes....

These whispering suspicions were terminated abruptly by a noise in the living-room, and Wentworth pressed his eyes to the peepholes which Hennessey used to spy on his baffled guests. It was the police who had invaded the penthouse, the building superintendent with them. He had unlocked the door and now stood by, watching wide-eyed, as they strode through the rooms and searched every possible hiding-place.

Wentworth tensed, but evidently the superintendent knew nothing about that chimney nook.

"There's nobody here," a sergeant reported to the lieutenant who had led the charge into Rockwell's apartment. "They must've gone downstairs instead of up."

"They're somewhere in this building," the fuming lieutenant growled, and started for the penthouse door. "They're still in the building. I'll find them if I have to take the damn place down brick by brick!"

Wentworth breathed more easily when the searchers had departed to carry out that laudable ambition. Again the penthouse was silent and in darkness. Twenty minutes passed, and they did nothing but shift positions in their cramped quarters.

Then once more there was a noise in the penthouse. This time it was Peter Hennessey. He strode into the living-room and flashed on the lights, to glance at his watch and then pace the floor nervously, back and forth, like an animal in a cage. For ten minutes he continued that restless pacing, while he lit and quickly discarded half a dozen cigarettes.

Then the phone rang, and he leaped to it.

"Hello." His voice sounded distinctly in the still room. "Yes—the building is full of policemen. They raided the Rockwell apartment and they have a body there—but I don't know who it is. I can't—I can't, I tell you!" Now he was excited, frantic. "I haven't anything more—I told you that yesterday. I'm broke, bankrupt—even worse."

He pleaded desperately. "I have done everything. I haven't gone back on you. What more can I do? You gave me your word that nothing would happen to her. I must know that she will be safe tomorrow night. Yes... yes—" Wentworth could see his face working, could see the desperation that flared in his eyes—"I can get one. I am in the reserve. I will be ruined if anything happens to it, or if you use it improperly—but I'll do it if you guarantee that she will be safe!"

His face was dripping with perspiration when the conversation ended and he sank back in his chair. For long minutes he slumped there, staring blankly into space, his handsome face haggard and stricken. Again he glanced at his watch and then turned on the radio.

A news broadcast had just begun, and the announcer's deep voice boomed from the speaker.

"This was one of the most brazenly daring raids in crime annals," he proclaimed. "Thirty-five drugstores of the Phelan chain were attacked simultaneously. In each case the procedure was the same. Customers and clerks were restrained from leaving, while a half-crazed victim of the mummy death invaded the store and filled the air with a pinkish vapor squirted from a metal container."

The announcer went on. "Those fumes were deadly. All who came in contact with the vapor were stricken. Five hundred and twenty new cases of the Withering Death have been taken to the hospitals, and all seem doomed by the baffling malady. However, there are at least two slight rays of hope in the evening's appalling tragedy. The authorities now know how the plague is communicated, and in one of the raids a prisoner was taken. He is Ram Singh, a Hindu in the employ of Richard Wentworth—for whose arrest ten thousand dollars in rewards have been posted."

Ram Singh captured! That meant that Nita must be in danger! Wentworth listened to that deep voice, and a full realization of the night's deviltry came to him. A mass raid by the dying mummies—a fiendishly conceived scheme for terrorizing the city. This was what Dr. Bradley had tried to tell him before the Sedgwick sanitarium came down on their heads. And that meant that Kenneth Rockwell must have known of that raid, must deliberately have taken Wentworth to the sanitarium, just after the mummies had left—just in time for the trap to close on him....

NOW IT was Wentworth who was on edge, frantically anxious to get out of this place and learn what had happened to Nita. It seemed that Peter Hennessey would sit there all night, staring into space—even after he had turned off the radio. But at last he picked up his hat and left.

Wentworth heard the penthouse door click shut, and then he

moved out of the cubbyhole. What had been the meaning of that telephone conversation? Half a dozen explanations suggested themselves, but there was no proof definitely to establish them. Quickly Wentworth strode to Hennessey's desk and went through its drawers. When he had finished, he had discovered a grisly mummy hand, a collection of bankbooks that indicated wholesale withdrawals during the past week, a life-insurance policy with a heavy loan entered against it....

Hennessey had been telling the truth over the phone—he *was* broke. But why? Evidently he was a victim of the terror, had been bled white by that threatening voice on the phone—or was there more to it than that? Was there another reason that would explain those mummies in the chimney recess?

Evidently something was due to occur the next night—something that should provide an answer for that question—but that was tomorrow, and the problem of the moment was to escape from that police-guarded building. From the edge of the roof Wentworth could see uniformed men posted at the foot of the fire-escape, now patrolling the front of the building. To attempt to leave by either of those exits would mean sure capture.

But there was another way. Wentworth remembered the wide-eyed superintendent... and he had the solution.

Cautiously he and Fogarty made their way downstairs, floor by floor, without interruption—to the basement. Warily they passed the boiler-room, stepped up to the superintendent's quarters—and jabbed an automatic into the man's back before he knew what was happening. He made no attempt to struggle but meekly submitted while they bound and gagged him, then ransacked his closets. They found two gray work-uniforms that would fit them, even though Fogarty's almost burst.

"All right," Wentworth clipped. "Now the barrels."

One after the other, they wheeled twenty cinder-filled ash drums out to the sidewalk, passed them right under the nose of a watching policeman—then stood mopping their brows before heading for the corner and a drink. Grinning, the cop watched them go. By the time the superintendent finally was discovered, Fogarty was on his way home to bed and Wentworth, divested of the uniform, was in a phone booth many blocks away.

"Dick—I'm *so* glad you called!" Nita almost sobbed her relief over the wire. "Ram Singh is in jail! Stanley would not listen— he insisted on taking him. But that isn't all. Doctor Rogers has been trying to reach you. His place was raided tonight by a gang of thugs. They wrecked everything—and he and Doctor Castleman barely escaped in time."

Rogers' little sanitarium wrecked! Wentworth's eyes slitted grimly, and his jaws clenched. The fiend behind the Withering Death was missing nothing. He seemed to have all-seeing eyes—and countless hands ready to strike out in half a dozen directions at once!

"They are at the Seminole Hotel now, in a suite where they are registered as Anderson and Marvin," Nita told him. "They are badly frightened and are waiting to hear from you."

Wentworth went to the Seminole at once, and found both Rogers and Castleman in a suite from which they did not dare stir. The Coast specialist was terrified, and out of his handbag he lifted the reason for his panic—a mummified hand.

"It came addressed to me this morning," he quavered, "and then tonight I was all but killed. Two of those thugs had me down on the floor, and I thought that would be my end. I—I think I *killed* one of them, Mr. Wentworth! I am not accustomed to violence—we do not have such flagrant law-breaking in California. I should never have come here, and now I want to get away at once. You brought me here and you must help me to leave. I am not safe anywhere in New York."

"I will take you to a place where you will be absolutely safe," Wentworth promised quickly. "My own place—where I guarantee nobody will be able to reach you. There you will be able to continue your work. You can't let them drive you out now when we need you so badly, Doctor."

"But your place, Wentworth?" Rogers made surprised protest. "How can you—with the police watching?"

HALF AN hour later he discovered how Richard Wentworth could enter and leave his Sutton Place stronghold even though a cordon of police surrounded it. From the Seminole, Wentworth taxied them across town to the East River and led the way to a low boat shed on a pier at Sixty-ninth Street. In that shed was a small, swift motor cruiser.

Silently it nosed out into the current.

Almost noiselessly the motor started turning and the tiny craft slipped through the darkness, making barely a ripple on the oily surface of the river. Under the Queensborough Bridge, and then close to the shore, to pick a way through a forest of slimy pillars—finally gliding up to a landing stage well hidden beneath a pier. That pier was one of the two on which part of the building at the water's edge rested.

Wentworth led the way along a cement corridor, into a basement room and to an elevator which shot them upstairs to his third floor living-room. Castleman was mute with amazement, but his round eyes missed nothing. Appreciatively they inventoried the well chosen furnishings of that luxurious room—when suddenly he staggered back as if stricken.

"There—there on that table!" he gasped and pointed tremblingly to an end table that stood in front of a wide casement window.

In the center of that table lay a mummified hand that seemed to be clutching for them!

Instantly Wentworth sprang across the room and lifted the grisly thing. Swiftly he cast about for a possible explanation. There was none. All six of the sections that composed the window were open a few inches—but nothing larger than a bird could have entered in that manner. There was no possibility that anybody could have reached the window from above or below to thrust or toss the thing inside—or any chance, either, that an intruder could have gotten into the building.

"It looks just like the other one," Castleman's trembling words came from between chattering teeth. "It *is!* They are mates!" as he took the hand that had been sent to him from his bag. "Mine is the right—and this is the left. It is meant for me—the second warning!" and his voice broke with fearful conviction of his own doom.

It was sometime before Wentworth could quiet him, but at

last Rogers and Castleman were assigned to rooms, and Wentworth came back to where Nita awaited him anxiously.

"This awful thing frightens me, Dick!" she half-whispered. "I don't feel safe—even here. Those ghastly hands seem to be able to reach in everywhere—and wherever they appear they bring death and frightfulness. Those poor people tonight in Phelan's—"

Quickly Wentworth told her what had happened to him that evening, ending with the perplexing climax in Peter Hennessey's penthouse apartment.

"Now I begin to see why Evelyn is so heart-broken," Nita said softly. "I could not understand why Peter Hennessey decided to stop backing her concert series. But if he hasn't the money of course he can't. Evelyn called me today and told me that her plans are all ruined. Instead of the series, there will be only one concert—the one tomorrow night. The money for that has all been paid. She asked me to attend, but with all this trouble—"

The concert tomorrow night! That must be what Peter Hennessey had been so concerned about! His anxiety was for Evelyn Marlowe—for fear she would not be safe when she stepped out into the glare of the footlights tomorrow night. A threat of some sort hung over Evelyn Marlowe, and tomorrow night, in the Randall's Island stadium, would bring it to a head....

"Perhaps it would be just as well if you do attend," Wentworth said thoughtfully. "Evelyn may need you—but I want you to take Jackson with you if you go."

Fifteen minutes later the dark-hulled little motor cruiser

nosed its way between the wet piles and out into the East River current. But now it had but one occupant. At the wheel Wentworth peered through the murky harbor gloom, but his mind was far from the stygian shoreline and the lapping wavelets— was busily planning for a showdown with the murdering master of the Withering Death!

If that fiendish mummy-maker was so anxious to come to grips with the Spider, the Spider would not disappoint him….

It was early the next day that Wentworth outlined his plan to Fogarty. The big detective chewed on his cigar butt as he listened, and a curious light came into the depths of his eyes.

"The Spider, eh?" he chuckled softly. "Well, I never thought *I'd* play *that* role. But if you say so, Wentworth…."

THAT NIGHT, he was all ready when the curtain went up in the crowded Randall's Island stadium, was at his place in a dark spot in the outdoor auditorium as the company made its first appearance. Wentworth had taken every precaution, locating these particular spots with the greatest of care. Before the lights were dimmed, he and Fogarty had paraded the aisles with baskets of refreshments. But the moment the illumination snapped off, their white uniforms disappeared, gave way to the Spider's ebon raiment. He and Fogarty were in place within easy reach of the stage and yet protected from inquisitive eyes that might have spotted them.

When the trouble started—

And then it did start! Just as Evelyn Marlowe came to the center of the stage for her first aria.

She was afraid, Wentworth saw that at once. Her eyes flashed around apprehensively, almost fearfully. Her rich soprano voice started to intone the aria—and then cloyed in her throat as she staggered backward her eyes turned upward in stark horror. For an instant she swayed there before she fell to the boards... and in that instant Wentworth spied the ghastly mummy hand that came down from the rim of the proscenium arch, lowered on an almost invisible cord, reaching for the prima donna.

In that instant the Spider went into action. His automatic cracked once, and that slender cord parted, the grisly hand plummeting to the stage—just as his twisted, stooping figure hurtled across the footlights and crouched over the gruesome object.

Pandemonium had already seized that vast crowd, but the Spider hovered before them. Raising his black-clad arms, like the wings of a huge bat, he called to them for silence. Above him he had located that cord, and located the spot behind the arch to which it ran. Then he leaped for it, clutched it in his hand and was tugging it down—to hover beneath it with his cape spread wide like a fireman's net.

Down from the rim of the archway came a round glass vessel, about the size and shape of the top unit of a drip coffeemaker—a stoppered glass container filled with a reddish liquid that looked like thinned blood!

Straight into that black cape the glass ball fell, and then the Spiders arms were wrapped around it, clutching it securely before it could crash to the stage floor.

"Stay where you are!" His cracked voice reached out to the terrified audience and held them spellbound. "The danger is past!" Now he clutched the severed mummy hand in one hand

and the glass vessel in the other, held them high. "You almost witnessed wholesale murder here this evening. If this glass container had crashed to the stage every man and woman in this opera company, and many of you in the audience besides, would have been stricken with the Withering Death!"

He went on. "But this cowardly mummy-maker forgot to reckon with the Spider—and this time he overreached himself! Now we have a specimen of his devilish poison. In another ten minutes the foremost scientists in America will be at work upon it. This fiendish murderer has terrified you long enough—now you have him licked, if only you will keep up your courage!"

Eerily his cackling laugh jangled and echoed through the great stadium—then suddenly he lifted the mummy hand above his head and flung it to the stage floor.

"We call your cowardly bluff, mummy-maker!" he hurled his defiance. "Now you are the one who will beg for mercy!"

CHAPTER 10
A SPIDER DIES

NITA VAN SLOAN was up out of her seat the moment Evelyn Marlowe staggered backward and fell to the stage floor. With Jackson close at her side, Nita hurried toward the rear of the stadium and the back-stage entrance. The prima donna was up before they reached her, already being led to her dressing room. But the moment she saw Nita the terror which threatened to prostrate her seemed checked. Instantly she was in Nita's arms, clinging to her, half-sobbing, half-imploring, as she urged the way to the street exit.

"Thank God you were out there, Nita!" she gasped. "You will know what to do—how to help me. But we haven't much time!" she glanced at her watch and terror flamed anew in her eyes. "We will be too late if we delay—we may even be too late already!"

"But where are we going?" Nita tried to calm the trembling girl.

"To Peter!" Evelyn gasped. "Oh, God—if we are too late!"

Frantically she led the way to the street and glanced around for a cab. Nita nodded to Jackson and he went for the car in which they had come to the stadium. Not until Evelyn Marlowe sank exhausted and quivering, onto its rear seat could Nita calm her to coherence.

"That awful hand!" Evelyn Marlowe shuddered. "I *knew* it would be there somewhere tonight. But I hoped against hope— told myself they wouldn't dare. But they *did* dare! They were able to reach me right out in front of all those people where I thought surely I would be safe!"

She admitted, when Nita questioned her, "No, this isn't the first time I have been threatened. For days I have been receiving threatening phone calls, but I haven't dared to tell anyone. I was warned that that would mean instant death for Peter. I have no idea who it is who has been calling me. At first he wanted money—far more than I could possibly hope to raise. And now he wants—*me*... Tonight he called again and warned me that this would be my last chance. If I did not obey this time, I would be responsible for turning Peter into a horrible mummy! And then that terrible hand came down to remind me that there is no escape!"

She shuddered. "I am going to him, Nita—it's all I *can* do. It's the only possible way I can save Peter from a terrible death. That voice on the telephone gave me an address on Park Avenue… where I must go if I am willing to meet his terms."

"And we are going there with you," Nita announced firmly. "Tell Jackson that address, and we will have a look at this brave gentleman."

The address Evelyn Marlowe gave was on lower Park Avenue, a four-story brownstone mansion that now appeared closed up. Nita glanced at the boarded windows, and the litter which had accumulated in the slightly recessed front court, and was certain that the call must have been a hoax. The building gave every evidence of having been closed for months, perhaps years. Yet Evelyn approached the lower door confidently. Her knock sounded hollowly in the still, deserted street.

Nita waited alertly, while Jackson, a few steps in the rear, stood with his hands clutching his pocketed guns. They were ready for anything that might come. But when it *did* come it was with such suddenness that they had no chance whatever.…

Twice Evelyn repeated that hollow knock on the boarded-up door—and then, without a warning sound, it was flung open and a horde of incredible-looking figures came leaping, swarming out of it. Before Nita could turn, she was overwhelmed. At the same instant, she saw something come hurtling down from overhead. One of those solid-board fronts swung back in place over the window it covered, as a dark figure leaped down and landed on Jackson's shoulders.

Jackson went down, but instantly was up on his knees, trying to scramble to his feet. He fought desperately, but he had no chance. Dazed, he could only half-defend himself against the attacker who clubbed at his head. Then they were all over him, dragging him down, pulling him inside the boarded-up door.

Nita endeavored to scream, but a horrible wrinkled hand clamped down over her lips. A dozen other hands seemed to have hold of her, then rushed her through a long, dark corridor, then down a flight of steps.

That nightmare trip terminated in what seemed to be an altogether barren cellar room. Two unshaded electric bulbs, set in the concrete ceiling, lit the place dismally. A chill trickled down her spine when she caught her first good look at her captors. Nearly a dozen of them—frightful, spectral-looking creatures, who were naked to the waist and seemed to be gaunt mummies! Terrible mummies who leered at them with obscene eyes that peered out of ghastly skeleton heads!

"Let me go!" Evelyn Marlowe panted, as she tried to fight her way through. "Let me go!" Her voice rose frantically as they blocked her on every side. "I have done my part—kept my bargain. Now let me go! You promised—"

But those leering faces mocked her.

Gaunt, dry-skinned arms closed around her, held fast. Wild fright flared in her eyes, and maddening terror transformed her face into a distorted mask, as she turned to Nita—then broke into hysterical gibbering.

"I tricked you—led you here deliberately! I had to do it, Nita!" she babbled wildly. "I couldn't stand the horrible thought of being turned into one of these terrible creatures—my body withered and shrunk like that! I *couldn't*, Nita—that was too awful! They told me that if I brought you here I would be spared! They promised—"

And then realization of the enormity of the thing that she had done swept over her, overwhelmed her.

"I know what I am—a coward, a betrayer!" she screamed wildly. "Tell me what you think of me, Nita! Tell me—I deserve it! But I couldn't let them do that to me! Forgive me for it, Nita—it was the only thing I could do to escape—and I did my part—"

"But you did it too late!" A deep, booming voice, that seemed to come from nowhere, suddenly filled the whole room and drowned her raving, dried up the babbling torrent from her trembling lips. "You took too long to make up your mind. Now it is too late. The hand of death has reached out—and grasped you. If you doubt that—*look at your skin!*"

Evelyn Marlowe held up her arm and stared at it unbelievingly. Suddenly all the color drained from her face, her eyes dilated, became wide saucers brim-full with horror—and a scream that was utter madness burst from her lips. Already darkening, her skin was becoming dry and papery, the skin of the mummy into which she was turning!

"Let that be a lesson to you, my dear Miss van Sloan," that booming voice chuckled a grim warning. "I do not countenance disobedience—not even for a few hours!"

WITH THAT precious glass container of mummy poison under his cape, the Spider whirled, gun in hand, and dived through the terror-chained backstage crowd before anyone could stop him. He had caught a glimpse of Nita making for the backstage and knew where she would go.

But when he reached Evelyn Marlowe's dressing-room it was empty.

Now the backstage force had recovered from their amazement, and the police were swarming to their aid. By the time Wentworth flung back from the star-marked door a crowd was surging threateningly up the corridor to cut off his escape.

"There he is!" someone yelled—and a bullet whistled by his head.

Wentworth did not dare trust the farther end of that corridor; it might lead him into a blind alley. He had to go back the way he had come—and there was only one way to do that. Grasping the poison-filled container, he whirled it over his head and charged. In wild panic they broke and fled the moment they comprehended that dread threat, ran frantically to cover—all except one stagehand who lost his footing in his frenzied haste.

He went down—and instantly the Spider was upon him, dragging him into a dressing-room, yanking off his overalls.

"That shirt and cap, too!" he snapped, as he leaped out of the black raiment and donned the terrified workman's clothes. His skilled fingers flew to his face and ripped off the ugly make-up. "Keep very quiet in here. Bolt the door and don't open it no matter how much they yell—if you want to live!" He flung this parting warning and sprang through the doorway, ducking and running as if he feared death would come hurtling after him at any second.

"He's back there—in that dressing-room!" he panted, as the others swarmed around him. "I just managed to slip out."

Then they were past him, were closing in warily on the closed door, the police circling it with ready guns and demanding the Spider's surrender.

"Marlowe's gone!" Wentworth heard the company manager excitedly shouting to a police captain above the din. "They kidnaped her—took her away in a car!"

Evelyn Marlowe had disappeared....

That meant that Nita, in all probability, was with her. They probably had gone off in the car Jackson was driving—but gone *where?*

In the washroom of a nearby tavern Wentworth discarded the stagehand's outfit and straightened his own rumpled clothing. A few moments more with his make-up kit, and he was ready to go back into the bar, step into a telephone booth and call Sutton Place.

But when he dialed the unlisted number there was no answer. Wentworth's nerves tingled with apprehension. Jenkyns was not at his post. That could have but one meaning—grave trouble. Nothing else could have induced the old man to leave his station when both Wentworth and Nita were away from the stronghold. Something was very wrong....

Now thoroughly alarmed, Wentworth hailed a cab and was driven to the East River pier where he kept the motor cruiser. But it was not there! Again that vague foreboding tingled through him, but this was no time to debate what might have happened to the cruiser. At the other end of the shed was a small canoe. Wentworth lifted it into the water and knelt in the bottom, sent it gliding noiselessly out into the river.

His broad shoulders swung the paddle, and the light craft sped over the water, skimming the surface with barely a sound— and, by that stillness alone, saved his life. His eyes were hardly accustomed to the darkness by the time he reached his own pier. But instinctively they picked out two small craft patrolling the river, with eyes as alert as his own.

Suddenly orange flashes blazed out in the darkness, and the sharp crack of automatics sped over the water. Wentworth dived low and gave the down-sweep that carried him into the protection of the pier-end.

Police—that must be the answer, he told himself grimly as he made the canoe fast and raced along the concrete passageway to the elevator. Kirkpatrick was leaving him no loophole, but bottling up every entrance to the building, determined to drive him out into the open. Somehow, the commissioner must suspect that he had been getting in despite the police guard posted on the streets....

WENTWORTH'S WHIRLING thoughts stopped short the moment he stepped into his sitting-room. Aghast, he stood in the doorway and stared at an incredible figure slumped in a chair beside the big center table. A weazened, shrunken figure in the black cape and floppy-brimmed hat of the Spider!

For an instant he poised, transfixed, then like a panther he catfooted up to the table. His darting eyes searched every corner of the room, his tense ears alert for the slightest tell-tale sound. But the room was empty, its only occupant that gruesome, silent figure at the table.

A gaunt, all-but-fleshless mummy, it sat there staring, hollow-eyed, at the table lamp less than two feet from its shrunken face. Unconsciously Wentworth's eyes followed that fixed gaze… and he felt the goose-pimples coming out on his arms.

Suspended by a tenuous strand from the edge of that lamp was a mossy-colored spider, its body covered with black spots. A giant species of tarantula that he placed at once as a native of Southern China; a species that grew to a body width of fully three inches. By the length of its legs he could tell that this specimen had been large—one of the largest of its kind. But now its furry legs were half-curled, its body shrunken.

It had been turned into a spider mummy!

Exactly as had that shrunken figure who sat staring sightlessly at it!

Instantly Wentworth realized the grim significance of this eerie tableau. The master of the mummy death had settled with the Spider—had left him there to die horribly, his doomed eyes fixed upon the insect from which he had taken his name!

The master of the mummy death had settled with the Spider—and it was Mike Fogarty who had died to settle the score! Mike Fogarty, who was to have followed any likely suspect from the Randall's Island stadium, and must have trailed his quarry here to Sutton Place—into a trap that had been baited for Wentworth himself….

Wentworth did not have to examine that incredibly shrunken

figure to know that life had departed. Fogarty's body had shriveled to less than a quarter of its ordinary girth. His thin, bony arms bound loosely to the chair that held him, the big detective was a mere shadow of his former self—and fastened into the withered skin of his emaciated throat were the bony fingers of a severed mummy hand, symbolically choking him to death!

Yet Fogarty still *lived!*

Wentworth beheld the wasted chest heave, the shriveled face twitch, the lips part. Instantly he fell to work at the ropes, slipping them off the desiccated arms, lifting Fogarty from the chair and carrying him easily to a nearby couch.

"No use," a voice that was nothing more than a whisper came from between the half-open lips. "Finished... nothing more. Came here... by boat. Followed man... from stadium. They were waiting... here."

He stopped, and for a moment it seemed that the whispering voice was stopped forever. Then a smile that was nothing more than a muscular grimace twisted those terribly weazened features, and Fogarty's dying eyes actually seemed to twinkle!

"I was always sure... you were the Spider," came barely audibly. "The world... needs you, Wentworth. I'm satisfied... good way to go...."

And then the shriveling jaws tightened, the gleaming eyes clouded and filmed over, and the loyal co-operator who had been Mike Fogarty was no more....

Stunned by the tragic loss of that faithful assistant, Wentworth stared down at the pitiful shell of a body, swathed in the far too roomy habiliments of the Spider. His strong hands balled into hard, white-knuckled fists. Mike Fogarty had gone to his death unafraid—but over his mummifying body Wentworth swore that he would not go unavenged!

Quickly he started to search the building, seeking a clue to the identity of Fogarty's murderers. But the stronghold he had considered so secure seemed deserted—until he discovered the body of Dr. Rogers lying on the floor in one of the upper rooms. The physician was unconscious, his head laid open by a nasty gash in his scalp. Swiftly Wentworth lifted him to a bed and washed the wound, dressed it as well as he could.

Rogers was still unconscious, but his pulse was beating regularly and he would soon recover. But of Orrin Castleman there was no sign. His room was empty, and the specialist seemed to have vanished. Snatched away by the murderers he had feared, the murderers who had done for poor Fogarty, Wentworth told himself bitterly. This stronghold which he had worked so hard to make impregnable had been nothing but a trap for all those caught in it....

That was when he reached the private garage, with its little rear cell that served as a telephone switchboard, and stared down at where old Jenkyns sprawled on the floor. At first glance he seemed dead—and in that moment Richard Wentworth's cup of bitterness was filled to overflowing. In that moment he seemed utterly alone.

Fogarty was dead, Ram Singh was in jail, Nita and Jackson had disappeared, Rogers was incapacitated—and now even old Jenkyns had been snatched away from him....

But Jenkyns was not dead. It was his pallor that made him

look like a corpse—and that probably had saved his life, Wentworth realized as he knelt beside the old butler. His attackers no doubt had left him for dead. But Wentworth lifted and carried him through the underground passage to the house, laid him on a bed and worked over him frantically.

Gradually a flush of color came back into the thin white cheeks. Jenkyns' pulse quickened, and then he opened his eyes.

"Castleman," he gasped as soon as he recognized Wentworth and could find his voice, "He was a *fake*, sir! He was a stooge planted here in the building to open it for his gang so that they could set a trap for you. The real Castleman is being held prisoner—that much I heard before they discovered me and knocked me out."

Castleman an impostor! That explained the raid on Dr. Rogers' sanitarium; explained the mummy hands which had trailed the supposed specialist; explained the missing motor cruiser....

Wentworth stood there trying to grasp the fact of the man's astonishing perfidy—when the telephone suddenly clamored. Wentworth reached for it instinctively, and then hesitated. Who could that be? Nita or Jackson would have called the garage number. Warily he lifted the receiver, and an excited voice came throbbing over the wire.

"Mr. Wentworth, is that you? Thank God, I have located you!" Austin Warrington panted. "I am trapped, and I don't know where to turn for help! Death is hanging over my head! I don't dare leave the house—but I know that even here my minutes are numbered! Help me, Wentworth—"

142

Suddenly the connection snapped off, and the line was dead.

CHAPTER 11
HORROR HUNT

T O ATTEMPT to run the water gauntlet outside the pier in a canoe would be even more dangerous than trying to escape from Sutton Place by land, now that those patrolling boats would be on the lookout for him. Wentworth considered quickly and made his decision.

A few minutes later, one of the row of private garages that bordered his property opened soundlessly, and a coupé rolled out and drove to the corner. Hunched behind the wheel, Wentworth expected at every moment to hear the bark of revolvers and the whine of leaden slugs. But nobody attempted to stop him. Without interruption he drove to East Thirty-sixth Street and drew up a few doors from Austin Warrington's home.

The street was deserted and utterly quiet, the old house somnolent, peaceful looking.

But Wentworth approached it alertly, his sharp eyes questioning every shadow, his muscles tense, ready to flex into whirlwind action at a moment's notice. Deliberately he thumbed the bell, and listened as its clatter echoed from within.

Peaceful—deceptively peaceful; and yet Austin Warrington's terror had not been without cause, and the abrupt termination of that phone conversation still remained to be explained.

Then the door was open and Wong, Warrington's valet, was standing in the entrance, his bland face half-interrogating as he regarded the face of Gordon Powell and failed to recognize Wentworth.

"Mr. Warrington desires to see Mr. Wentworth," the unfamiliar visitor smiled, and Wong's dark eyebrows raised in surprise.

A few moments later he led the way to Warrington's study, but now Wentworth was close at his back, fairly treading on his heels as they stepped into the lighted room where the scientist sat at his desk and looked as if he expected death to snatch him at any moment.

Warrington's cheeks were blanched, ashen-white. The fingers of his right hand picked nervously at his desk-blotter, while his left clenched and unclenched continually on the arm of his chair. His eyes gleamed with terror, and his lips moved soundlessly before he could speak.

"I would not have recognized you, Mr. Wentworth," he managed at last, "but I suppose I should have expected—"

But Wentworth was paying no attention. His glance had flashed from Warrington to the valet—and had caught the sudden gleam of excitement that lit the Oriental's eyes. Just for a second—but that second was sufficient to sound a warning in Wentworth's brain. Something was afoot in that house... something that was going to break at any moment!

Warned by that give-away flash, he dodged just in time—ducked to one side as a heavy-set man leaped out at him from behind a standing screen. That fellow had "cop" written all over him, Wentworth saw at a glance, even as his fist swung up and smashed against the big man's jaw. He went down like a log, but instantly two others seemingly materialized from nowhere to take his place—and behind them was Stanley Kirkpatrick, stern-faced and grim-lipped.

A trap! Kirkpatrick had baited this trap for him!

Wentworth's eyes narrowed. He saw Austin Warrington backing away fearfully, caught a glimpse of Wong's slant-eyed face as the Oriental hovered on the edge of the fray—and then those department huskies were closing in on him from two sides. Wentworth backed warily. Then a blackjack whipped through the air and smashed down on his left shoulder, almost paralyzed his whole arm. He caught the glint of light on a revolver barrel, and remembered Kirkpatrick's reward offer.

Dead or alive! So that was it… Wentworth toppled sidewise, started to go down—then suddenly a heavy chair was in his hands, was sailing across the room to catch that third cop full in the chest. The revolver roared harmlessly and went skittering into a corner, and Wentworth whirled to confront the blackjack-wielder. In mid-swing he caught the fellow's arm, placed a hand behind his shoulder, twisted quickly—and sent him sailing head over heels through the air, to crash in a heap at Kirkpatrick's feet.

Before the cursing cops could organize and close in again on their elusive adversary, Warrington's desk rose and toppled on one side—and crouched behind it, confronting them over the steady muzzles of two automatics, was the man they knew was Richard Wentworth.

"You ought to know better than this, Kirk," he chided, and his grin was steel-hard. "A fine way to have men seriously injured in performance of their duty—but it's Warrington I want to have a

The Chinese came at him with a rush, as he whipped out his guns!

word with. What is the meaning of this treachery, Warrington?" he whirled savagely to where the old man cowered against a bookcase.

"I COULD not help myself!" Warrington pleaded abjectly, and from the way he trembled Wentworth judged that he was on the verge of nervous prostration. "They demanded that I trick you into coming here so that the police could take you. Either that or they threatened me with the same terrible fate they dealt to my daughter—to turn me into a mummy...."

"They? Who do you mean by 'they?'" Wentworth flashed at him.

"How do I know!" the old man flung up his hands hopelessly. "A voice on the telephone and then one of those terrible mummy hands. You know how the whole city has been terrified—how helpless the police have been. I have been threatened a dozen times, and today I received *this*."

Tremblingly he held out a folded note. "I found that lying here on my desk, clutched in a severed hand just like the one that spelled my Susan's doom. I knew that it meant my death unless I obeyed, Wentworth."

But Wentworth hardly heard him. Unbelievingly his blue-gray eyes were staring at that slip of paper, were reading the brief message that promised Warrington certain death unless he obeyed the orders he had received. But even those threatening words meant little compared to the handwriting that had delineated them. Wentworth knew that handwriting; he had seen specimens of it recently, and was certain that it was Kenneth Rockwell's!

Kenneth Rockwell's handwriting....

More than ever, as Wentworth stared down at that familiar script, he felt that he was completely enmeshed in a web of treachery. On every side he was buffeted by wild currents of helpless, unreasoning terror.

Patsy DeLott had died a broken man, his power wrecked by the terror that dominated him.... John Gregg had died with unknown fear hanging over his head. Peter Hennessey had cowered in terror at his telephone. Austin Warrington stood there now on the brink of collapse with terror dancing in his eyes. And Kenneth Rockwell....

Wentworth had come to the conclusion that young Rockwell, also, had betrayed him because of the terror that hung over him. But this note—was it irrefutable proof of Rockwell's guilt or was it another evidence of the length to which a man's terror would drive him?

Over the barrels of his leveled automatics Wentworth pondered that question—and once more he caught the slant-eyed gaze of Wong, the Oriental, upon him.

There was something strangely familiar about the man's face. Wentworth knew that he had seen it somewhere—but where?

Wong, a Chinese. Into Wentworth's mind flashed a memory of that shrunken spider in front of Mike Fogarty's drying eyes—a Chinese spider... Henry Mallon's chauffeur had been a Chinese also... And those disemboweling cuts that had ended the lives of Mallon and Gregg—they were typically Chinese, not like the throat-slitting of Latin-blooded gangsters. Typically Chinese—just like the reckless sacrifice of that killer who had yielded his own life in a desperate attempt to blow up the cab in which Wentworth and Ted O'Neill were riding.

That array was far too long for mere coincidence. As incident piled on incident Wentworth felt his blood leap with the excitement of a fresh, hot lead. A lead that he knew how to follow. For in that moment he remembered where he had seen Wong, recalling a hop-joint tucked away in the cellars of the East Side where the denizens of New York's underworld mingled with the sons of China.

"Drop your guns on the floor, *carefully,*" he snapped at the red-faced officers. "Remember, Kirk—it was you who gave this 'dead or alive' order. That leaves me no choice. Gather them up, Wong," as the revolvers thudded to the carpet. "Now remove their belts—and be careful that you do not step in front of them. Strap their hands tight at their sides."

The three fuming policemen, Kirkpatrick and Warrington—one by one Wong strapped them up, and then stood silently while Wentworth trussed him in similar fashion. That makeshift tethering would hold them only a little while, Wentworth knew, but he needed only time to get out of the building and reach his car at the curb.

Straight downtown he drove, until he turned in at a public garage several blocks from Holian Alley and left the machine there.

HOLY ALLEY seemed deserted when he approached it on foot, but he knew that deceptive appearance of emptiness; knew that sharp eyes would scrutinize every intruder. Instead of entering Number One, he turned into Pallin Place and slipped into the entrance of the building which backed onto the one in which Blinky McQuade had his room. Through a gloomy hallway, across a dimly lit triangle of communal backyard—and he was in the Holian Alley hallway, was unlocking Blinky's hideout.

Five minutes later it was Blinky McQuade who shuffled out into Holian Alley and mingled with the shadows that always lay heavy there. The length of the alley and then eastward into a section that was even more congested than his own, he went, to turn suddenly and duck down into a basement Chinese laundry. Past the two stolid Cantonese who labored at ironing-boards, through a curtained doorway into a dim hallway that led downward—and he stood in the pitch-black anteroom of China Sam's.

From out of the darkness came a warning sound. A light snapped on, and behind it was dimly visible a hulking, broad-shouldered figure with hands folded into the broad sleeves of a silken jacket—a pock-marked Chinese who smiled blandly when he recognized his visitor.

"Long time no see," he grinned, and then his quick, beady eyes caught the suppressed excitement in Blinky's face. "You come now for special reason?" he hazarded.

"Damn right, Sam." Blinky growled. "I gotta see you alone—gotta see you quick, understand? Somethin' here." He nodded to his grimy coat pocket. "I wanna show you—somethin' that'll open your eyes."

China Sam beamed, and he led the way into the silk-curtained cubbyhole that was his private office. His dark, slitted eyes glanced at Blinky's pocket expectantly—and popped wide open when a brownish, mummified hand dropped onto his desk and slid toward him.

"There it is, Sam," Blinky gritted, and the automatic he gripped was thrust deep into the Chinese's ample paunch. "No use tryin' to call any of your China-boys—I'll let you have it through the belly before they can bring me down. I wanta know what you know about those mummy hands."

"Nothing," China Sam protested in a voice that came like the low hiss of a snake. "I know nothing, foolish one—"

But Blinky's free hand darted out, groped beneath the silken jacket and came out again with a keen-bladed knife. He turned its needle point against the dive-keeper's middle.

"All right, maybe this'll help you to open up," he snarled as the point bit through the thin silk garment and began to stain it crimson. "I wanta go to this mummy dive—and you're takin' me, Sam."

That first off-guard flash in the Chinese's eyes, when he had been confronted with the severed hand, told Blinky that he was on the right track. Now he pressed the knife mercilessly. China Sam's yellow face beaded with perspiration, deadly hate gleamed from his eyes—but he capitulated.

"Only a fool seeks his own death," he rasped, "but I take you to yours—with happiness!"

Warily Blinky watched him until they were out on the street, but China Sam took no chances with the gun muzzle now trained on his ribs. Silently he led the way eastward into the narrow streets of Chinatown, to a novelty bazaar that was owned by Chen Ah-lo, one of the Oriental colony's foremost citizens.

The bazaar was closed, but China Sam went to a door at one side of the showroom, opened it and stepped into a close, stagnant-smelling hallway.

"And now where?" Blinky demanded suspiciously, and his ready gun jabbed close.

"We go right," the Chinese said sourly. "There is a stairway at the end of the hall. We go to the floor below—"

"Not you, Sam," Blinky corrected. "This is as far as you go—right here. I want that outfit of yours—pants, jacket, cap, shoes—the whole thing. Get out of them quick."

Stripped of his outer clothing, China Sam glared his venomous hatred while Blinky bound and gagged him securely, then dragged him down the corridor to where some of Chen Ah-lo's empty packing-cases were piled. With the Chinese safely hidden beneath these, Blinky got busy with his make-up kit and worked until his frowsy face had given way to a smooth, round-cheeked Oriental countenance.

This disguise brought him within reach of the guard at the door of the downstairs rooms—and his automatic accomplished the rest. Before the suddenly suspicious Oriental could sound an alarm, the weapon came down over his head. Wentworth caught him as he slumped, dragged him to one side and bound and gagged him as securely as China Sam.

CAUTIOUSLY HE catfooted along the narrow corridor beyond the anteroom in which the guard had met him. It opened into a large, drapery-hung chamber that looked as if it was a temple—and here luck was with Wentworth. The only illumination came from dim lanterns, so weak that he could barely distinguish the score or more of men who were gathered around a large lacquer table in its center.

Wentworth slipped in without difficulty, kept well in the shadows, and worked his way to within twenty feet of the assemblage. Now he could clearly distinguish the round, fat face of Chen Ah-lo, could hear him haranguing the gathering in Cantonese.

"The white men did nothing to help us when we needed them so badly," the singsong denunciation flowed from his lips. "They turned a deaf ear and allowed China to perish. But China is not dead—the dragon never dies. Soon there will be a reawakening. China will rouse from her sleep and cast off the shackles Japan fastened upon her."

A low, passionate rumble of endorsement interrupted him, and Wentworth saw the fanatical fervor in many of those slant-eyed listeners.

"But that depends upon you," Chen Ah-lo whipped at them swiftly. "Without gold there is no hope. But China will have gold"—his smile was bland, complacent—"provided by these white men who deserted her in her time of need. Already the fund is growing, my brothers. Millions of dollars are pouring into it daily through your efforts. But we must not stop now. We must drain every dollar while there is still time."

Keenly Wentworth studied those avid faces. Most of the listeners, he saw, were young men—poor, misguided dupes being led into atrocious crimes under the guise of patriotism. But among them were others—sly-eyed men who watched them calculatingly, with evil satisfaction. Worst of all was the cunning Chen Ah-lo.

"Tomorrow morning we will strike our greatest blow. The very heavens will be filled with the death of the mummy, and the last thought of resistance to our demands will have been swept away. Knickerbocker Village will be the greatest field of battle in all China's glorious history!" he exulted. "You all know your duties for tomorrow. Let me remind you only of this—for failure the only excuse is death."

That terminated his harangue and was the signal for the meeting to disband. By ones and twos they left, until there remained only half a dozen who still conferred with Chen Ah-lo. One of those Wentworth recognized now—the chauffeur who had driven for Henry Mallon!

And then another arrived—another whom he knew well. There in the doorway was Wong, Austin Warrington's valet, with the raging China Sam at his side!

"A snake hides here in the darkness!" the Chinese shouted. "A white snake who is called Blinky McQuade. He tricked me—"

But at the first sound of alarm Chen Ah-lo had sprung back and pressed a wall button. Instantly lights flashed on in every corner of the big room—lights that illuminated the place brightly, and made Wentworth's hiding-place untenable. Narrow, hate-filled eyes spied him, glared malevolently—and then the Chinese came at him in a rush.

Wentworth whipped out his guns, but even before he could pull the triggers they were wrested from his hands. Yellow-skinned men leaped at him from every side and carried him to the floor. Clutching hands tore at his throat, sharp knives gleamed above him, sought his flesh hungrily. Twisting and squirming out of their clawing hands, he seized one of his adversaries and lifted him as a shield—heard the fellow scream as the knives of his mates stabbed into him. Throwing the wounded man clear, Wentworth came up from the floor like a suddenly released spring.

That frantic leap carried him clear across the room to where Chen Ah-lo was watching with raging eyes. Savagely Wentworth lashed out at the fellow, just managed to reach him—then was pulled down from behind and overwhelmed.

"Be careful of him!" he heard the big man's voice shout above the tumult. "Be very careful that no knife reaches his heart. I have other plans for him. For tonight and tomorrow he will wait and contemplate what is to happen to him—and then he will pay for this intrusion. Take him away—until tomorrow!"

Chen Ah-lo clapped his hands, and Wentworth was picked up bodily and carried out of the room, down another flight of steps and to a prison cell that had been hewn out of Manhattan's native rock. A cell without window or light—with nothing but a heavy, iron-barred door....

FOR HOURS he sat on the cold floor of that damp, clammy dungeon, vainly endeavoring to conjure up some magic plan that would affect his release. So this was the explanation of the Withering Death—a diabolical Oriental plot, the fiendish scheming of a wily Chinaman using his own people to wring a stupendous fortune from helpless victims! The men of Chen Ah-lo's race knew well the tremendous power of terror. For centuries they had utilized terror to intimidate and punish their enemies—and now Chen Ah-lo had turned it loose on New York in its most ghastly form.

Over the heads of rich and poor, powerful and lowly, gangster and police official, he held the threat of a fearful mummy death—a threat he had not hesitated to carry out whenever required by his evil purpose.

Tomorrow morning, it now seemed, would witness the frightful climax of that reign of terror—the final, all-demoralizing demonstration of ruthless ferocity that would wipe out the city's last resistance. Tomorrow morning—and in some way that demonstration was to be tied up with Knickerbocker Village, the huge apartment-house development within a stone's throw of Chinatown.

What appalling form that culminating outrage would take Wentworth could not guess. But before his mind's eye floated visions of thousands of terror-stricken citizens fleeing for their lives, droves of innocent victims stricken and shrieking in agony as their bodies shriveled and became gaunt mummies. The mummy death on a larger scale than the stunned city had yet endured... and he was penned up here in this dungeon, helpless to interfere.

Hour after hour of thoughts that were like the red-hot torture irons of the Inquisition—and with each hour the knowledge that the awful doom that hung over those unsuspecting victims was drawing near....

Wentworth felt over every square inch of that stone cell, but there was not the slightest break in those solid walls; not the slimmest chance of opening that solid door. A man immured in this dark hole might be left here for years, for generations, and nobody on the streets high above would have the slightest suspicion.

But he would not be left here to rot.

Chen Ah-lo had other plans for him—devilish plans to be carried out the next day. It was already the next day—well on in the morning, he saw as he held a match to his watch. Nearly nine o'clock, and Chen Ah-lo's unholy plans must be well under way....

SUDDENLY WENTWORTH tensed, and the match dropped from his fingers.

He listened again. Someone was coming down to him at last—someone who might open that cell door... and might come sufficiently close to the bars so that he could be grabbed and pulled against them.

Close beside the cell doorway Wentworth waited. Now he could see a light approaching. It was a lantern, carried by a Chinese. The fellow came up to the cell and put the lantern on the floor, turned a big key in the rusty lock and started to open the door—and then Wentworth had him.

Leaping from the doorway like a tiger, he carried the man backward, swept him off his feet and dashed him to the floor. Wentworth's fingers closed around his throat and pounded his head against the hard floor.

The fellow was struggling desperately for air, was trying to say something—and then he managed to tear his lacerated throat free.

"Blinky!" he gasped. "Geez—lay off before you strangle me! I come down here to get you out."

That voice was familiar. Wentworth relaxed his grip ever so little and peered down at his captive—the thin face of Dopey Weasel!

"Hell!" Dopey wheezed as he massaged his neck. "You almost croaked me! Fine way to treat a guy for trying to give you a hand. I saw you with China Sam last night and followed you to see what you were up to," he confided as Wentworth released and helped him to his feet. "I was in the big room upstairs when they jumped you—but there wasn't anything I could do but lay low and wait for my chance. That didn't come till a little while ago. Then I knocked out your jailer and took his place."

He confirmed Wentworth's fears.

"There's gonna be hell popping any minute now, Blinky. Far as I can make out, they're gonna blow hell out of Knickerbocker Village—but I can't do anything about that. I learned something in here last night that I been trying to find out ever since Sue— well, ever since this mummy scare began. And now that I know it, I wouldn't waste another minute if I knew the whole city of New York was gonna be blown to hell!"

His voice shook with emotion, and Wentworth saw his eyes blaze madly as he lifted the lantern and started up the corridor.

"We're not out of here yet," he warned glumly as they reached the foot of the steps. "We're gonna hafta battle our way out of this joint. That's why I came down after you—not because I'm sold on you, but because two of us got a better chance than one."

Even before they reached the big temple room that prediction was fulfilled. Above them Wentworth heard excited voices, calling out in Cantonese, heard footsteps padding toward the head of the stairs—and then he charged. Like a rocket he leaped up the steps and pitched into half a dozen Orientals who had already gathered there.

Three of them his flailing fists cleared from his path, and then the others were on top of him, were bearing him down. But he *couldn't* be knocked down! He *couldn't* be stopped now! The lives of hundreds, perhaps thousands, of helpless men, women and children depended on him getting out of that place!

Somehow he fought back onto his feet.

He got his hands on a long, wicked-looking knife—a knife that began to drip with blood when he used it as a scythe to clear the way across that big room and to the doorway beyond. Dopey Weasel was close behind him when they erupted from the floor below. Wentworth heard his automatic blazing and caught a glimpse of him as he laid about him in every direction with the weapon's bloodied barrel.

But after that he lost sight of the man.

He thought only of getting away—for the sake of those helpless ones whose lives depended on him!

Somehow he fought his way up the last stairway and staggered groggily through the corridor to the street door beside Chen Ah-lo's bazaar. Only then did he realize that the Weasel was no longer with him—and then it was too late to attempt to return and rescue the man. It would be hopeless suicide, a thing he had no right to attempt when so many other lives might depend on what he did in the next few minutes.

Already the morning was speeding past, the sun well up.

Not until he stared out into the bright sunshine did he realize his appearance—that he was clad in the tatters of a silken Chinese costume and gripped a bloody knife almost as long as a sword. Swiftly he stripped off China Sam's ruined garments and restored the frowsy countenance of Blinky McQuade. Then while his flying fingers worked, his whirling brain did its best to figure where Dopey Weasel could possibly fit into that strange pattern of crime the papers called the Withering Death….

CHAPTER 12
VILLAGE OF DEATH

THE MOMENT he could leave the doorway in which he had taken refuge for his lightning transformation, Wentworth made a bee-line for the nearest telephone booth and called police headquarters. Kirkpatrick must be warned of the danger which hung over Knickerbocker Village… But the commissioner had left his office and his assistants did not know where to locate him.

"Knickerbocker Village?" the voice on the other end of the wire became vibrant with interest the moment Wentworth tried to give his warning. "What do you know about trouble in Knickerbocker Village? Wait a minute, hold the line till I get a pencil. I want to take this down—"

But that feeble pretext was far too flimsy. Wentworth knew that the fellow was already barking orders over another wire and that in a few moments radio cars would be converging on that telephone to pick him up. Inwardly raging against such departmental stupidity, he hung up the receiver and quickly left the store.

Again Kirkpatrick's men had failed when their help was so sorely needed. Instead of listening and taking swift action on the warning he could give, they must insist on dragging him down to headquarters for a cross-examination—waste precious minutes in talk while countless lives might hang in the balance!

Subconsciously Wentworth's angry footsteps had turned toward the great model apartment structure that had replaced two square blocks of the worst tenement district in Manhattan. It was Sunday, he realized, as he noticed the number of people in the streets—but even that did not account for the excited crowds that almost blocked his way as he neared the big apartment house.

The sidewalks, even the gutters, were jammed—and yet the wide-eyed onlookers held aloofly back from the immediate vicinity of the huge Village quadrangle. Excited onlookers who obviously were expecting something to happen—and were poised, ready to flee, at a moment's notice.

Wentworth worked his way through them until the apartment building loomed just ahead. The streets immediately adjoining it were almost deserted. Around Knickerbocker Village the police had drawn a cordon through which none but tenants were allowed to penetrate—but nobody else seemed anxious to pass the bluecoats who barred every entrance.

"Not me—you couldn't pay me to go in there!" one of Blinky's barroom acquaintances answered his query of what it was all about. "They been warned that they hadda pay, but they think they can get away with holding out. After what that mummy hand outfit's been doing in this town? I'm mighty glad I don't live in that dump today, I tell yuh!"

Blinky shuffled past on the side of the street opposite the police-ringed building—and through one of the main entrances he could see the crowd of tenants who thronged the inside quadrangle. Hundreds of them, they were milling around a huge wooden placard that had been erected in the center of the grounds. What that placard announced he could not read, but he soon found plenty of others who could tell him.

"It's from the Withering Death," a wide-eyed taxi-driver told him hoarsely. "I was in there right after they found the thing—before the cops come and chased out anybody who don't live there. It tells 'em that the outfit that runs the buildings refused to pay their insurance and now the tenants has to pay it themselves. There's a picture of one of them mummy hands painted at the bottom of it."

A warning from the master of the Withering Death that he intended to collect "insurance" directly from the tenants… Wentworth remembered the evil, sing-song prophecy that had come from the lips of Chen Ah-lo, and his heart chilled as he wondered how payment was to be exacted….

Now he was conscious of eyes upon him, watching him intently. Not from the buildings of Knickerbocker Village, but from the tenements at his back. Slowly he turned, and for a moment his gaze clashed with that of Lefty Lomack, where the gangster leaned against the bar in a corner tavern. A cruel, wolfish half-grin wreathed the killer's face—and in the same moment Wentworth caught the gleam of metal in that saloon, the flash of light on unsheathed guns!

The police were there to see that none but tenants entered the Village limits—and the gangsters were there to see that the tenants did not leave—were there to keep them penned in their apartments to await God only knew what fate!

SOMETHING OF that knowledge must have penetrated to the tenants in the big inner court. Now Wentworth could see that they were swarming to the entrances, arguing with the blue-coats who tried to hold them back. A woman screamed shrilly.

"Back into your apartments!" a raucous voice bellowed above the turmoil. "This is just a trick to get us all out here in the open where we can be bombed!"

Bombed! That terrifying word turned their eyes upward to scan the sky for possible danger, and then sent them storming back through the building doorways—only to be met by the frantic hundreds now trying to fight their way out.

Richard Wentworth listened to that uproar and realized all too well what it meant. Terror had been insidiously planted there in that quadrangle—terror now spreading like wildfire. That threatening sign had whispered of death that hung over them, and in their frantic efforts to escape, the miserable tenants were rushing straight into the chill arms that opened for them.

Already women and children were being trampled underfoot, killed, in the insane scramble. And if a plane should appear in the sky there would be no possible chance of controlling the frenzied riot....

A plane… Someone must have spread that terrifying rumor among the trapped tenants—someone who was deliberately preparing them for the greater tragedy still to come! Again Wentworth could hear Chen Ah-lo's chuckling promise of death that would rain from the heavens—*death that would come down from a plane!*

Wentworth realized, in a sudden horror of understanding, this must have been the meaning of the telephone conversation he had overheard in Peter Hennessey's penthouse apartment. Young Hennessey had said that he belonged to the reserve—the Army Aviation Reserve! It was a plane that he had promised to secure for whoever was threatening him on the other end of that line—an Army plane to rain death upon this helpless multitude penned up in the great Knickerbocker Village quadrangle!

That was to be Che Ah-lo's masterstroke—a cold-blooded slaughter of thousands of innocent people whose only offense was that their landlord had refused to pay tribute!

Fearfully Wentworth turned his eyes skyward. The blue heavens were still empty. But now it seemed that every window in that great apartment structure was thronged with frightened faces. Sunday, when few of the tenants were away at work—that accounted for all those faces, and revealed how cunningly the merciless fiend had planned to miss nothing that would add to the appalling horror now to be flaunted in the face of a cringing city!

Now it seemed that every eye was turned upward, searching the cloudless sky. The tenants in the quadrangle, at the apartment windows, the police, the crowds outside in the streets—all were craning their necks. Wentworth knew that Chen Ah-lo's agents were doing their work exceedingly well. Everywhere people were waiting, waiting with helpless, horrible fascination....

But there must be some way to stop this ghastly mass-execution!

There *was* a way—a way that was fraught with death, a way that would plunge him straight into the grave! But it was the *only* way—and with the lives of these helpless thousands at stake Richard Wentworth knew that he could not turn his back upon it.

BURROWING HIS way to the rear of that ever-increasing crowd, he hailed the first taxi he met and gave the driver the address of his Sutton Place residence. Police or no police, he must get into that building—and without delay. Busily his brain wrestled with the problem, and before the cab turned into Sutton Place he had the answer.

Off the Place and into a side street he directed the cabbie. Now he could see two uniformed men on guard at the entrance to his grounds just across the way from where the taxi stopped.

"This the place, boss?" The driver turned around doubtfully.

"Yeah," Wentworth grunted, and leaned close to peer at the meter through Blinky's metal-hooded spectacles. "Hell!" he exploded, the moment he saw the clocked figure. "Whadda you think I wanna do—buy the heap? You got a fat chance of gettin' that, bud."

The cabbie protested, but Blinky's snarl became threatening, and his hand started toward his hip pocket. The driver waited for no more. Leaping from his seat, he ran, yelling wildly for help, to the bluecoats.

They listened to his excited tirade and started toward the cab. But the moment the cabbie had quit his seat, Wentworth had flung himself behind the wheel. Clapping a small pitch-pipe to his lips, he blew on it three times, three scaled notes—and the sonic-operated gates in the high wall swung open. With a snort the cab left the curb, almost knocked the cops and the anguished driver off their feet, and swung through the gates which closed silently behind it.

Wentworth tucked a twenty-dollar bill beneath the meter flag as he leaped from the cab. Police whistles were shrilling out on the street, as he raced for the ground-level doorway of the river-edge building and let himself in. Blue-coated figures were boosting one another over the wall when he pressed a button which sealed that entrance with a barrier of inch-thick steel.

That would hold them and give him ample time to reach the elevator which dropped him to the subterranean passages that underlay the entire building.

This time he did not head for the end of the pier he had used before. Instead, he hurried to the farther end of the basement, where the other pier reached out into the river.

But this was not an actual pier. It was a dummy—a concrete tunnel camouflaged on the outside with thickly planted piles. A tunnel which sloped downward so that there were several feet of water at the bottom of its river end. In that little basin lay cached what Wentworth wanted—a trim little Seversky Amphibian plane that was painted as black as night.

Quickly he climbed into the cockpit, and threw on the starter. The motor roared to life. He listened to its smooth hum, then reached out to push a button that would open the soundproof chamber. Down into the river mud sank the whole front of the pier, and the seaplane glided out onto the river in a beautiful arc that carried it into the sky.

Straight downtown he headed, his goggled eyes peering ahead of him, expecting at every moment to see what he dreaded.

And there it was!

High above the great quadrangle of Knickerbocker Village hovered an Army bombing plane of the ground-strafing variety! WENTWORTH'S JAWS clenched, and he gave the Seversky all the gas the motor would take. Yet he felt with sickening certainty, that he was too late. The bomber was spiraling upward, gaining altitude for a power-dive. He could not possibly reach it in time to prevent the loosing of the cargo of death it would send hurtling into the quadrangle.

Now it had reached a good three thousand feet, was leveling out, banking—and then it went plummeting downward like a comet. Straight at that green quadrangle which was rimmed on every side by the solid walls of the apartment buildings; straight down into what seemed an inevitable crash—but at the zero moment the pilot pulled it out of the very jaws of death. Up it swung—and out from beneath it dropped a black bundle.

Wentworth clapped a pair of binoculars to his eyes and tensed for the roar of the devastating explosion. But he saw that the plummeting object was no aerial bomb. It was a body—a body suspended from a parachute that blossomed open above it. A terribly emaciated body—but one that would be recognized by everyone who saw it.

Clad in the flowing costume of Aida that she had worn for her Randall's Island stadium debut, the mummified body of Evelyn Marlowe was making a ghastly entrance before a terror-bound audience!

Now Wentworth's plane was almost above the stricken apartment development, gliding downward in a trajectory that would almost cut off the climbing bomber. Within less than fifty feet they passed each other, and he caught a glimpse of four gas-masked, strangely clad men in the bomber's cabin. Three of them were at work with huge tanks, which they were lashing in position to up-end. Tanks loaded with frightful death—that was the meaning of those gas-masks and the rubbery-looking coveralls the four were wearing as protection from the fatal mummy liquid to be spilled into the quadrangle!

It was the Withering Death that would deluge Knicker-bocker Village from the very heavens!

In the flash of a split-second the bomber was past, but Wentworth veered and sent the Seversky soaring after it. Around and around the larger machine he flew, a little black spider matched against a huge hornet, trying desperately to drive the death-laden monster off its course and away from the doomed thousands who cowered below it.

But that hornet could sting. Guns blazed from its cabin, and lead sieved through the spider's black wings, tore through the fuselage and threatened to smash the controls. Grimly Wentworth bent low behind the cowl and dived straight at his adversary. Three times he drove the murder-plane off its course, but now they were flying low—so low that he could see the hell that was raging below.

The appearance of Evelyn Marlowe's mummified body had snapped the last vestige of control, down there in the huge apartment house. Wildly the frantic tenants had fled from the open court, taking refuge in the buildings or endeavoring to fight their way out into the streets. The police gave ground before this wave of terror-maddened men and women—but beyond the blue cordon were the guns of Lefty Lomack's waiting killers.

Tommy-guns blazed from windows and doorways, swept the sidewalk around each entrance and drove the panic-stricken victims back. A ring of flame and lead circled and held them there to await doom. But even the deadly hazard of those gangster guns was as nothing compared to the dread doom that threatened from above.

To die was one thing, but to be turned into horrible mummies….

Out of the windows the frenzied victims hurled themselves in a frantic effort to reach the street before they were trapped in their apartments. High above the fiendish trap, Wentworth caught snatches of their fearful screams, saw their bodies plunging downward—to land on the sidewalk with bone-shattering force. Most lay where they fell, some managed to get back on their feet and to stagger a few steps before a deadly blast of lead caught and mowed them down.

Helpless human beings penned up like condemned rats in a trap! Death awaited them everywhere they turned!

THE WITHERING DEATH

WENTWORTH'S GREAT heart ached for them, red rage fogged his vision—and he dived straight at the oncoming bomber. If he could crash into the machine, at least that menace would be ended. But the bomber's pilot dipped low just in time to avoid the collision—and clearly visible now was one of those deadly tanks poised on the cockpit's rim.

There would be death in every square inch of that pink mist—ghastly, incredibly horrible death. And Wentworth could not stop it. Vainly he had turned his automatics on the bomber. They were ineffectual even when they found their elusive mark—and now the murder-plane was power-diving again. He could see the gas-masked devils gripping the tank.

But this time he would not fail!

Side-winging into a hairpin turn, he flattened out and dove directly into its path, dipping low, so that the pilot would have no chance to slip under him. Down—down! The city roofs were rushing to meet him, but so was that death-laden plane. Down—down! And then, little more than five hundred feet from the ground, they met almost head-on!

For a fraction of a second that seemed an eternity Wentworth saw the down-roaring bomber right in front of him, could almost feel the terrific impact—as he yanked the lever that dropped the seat out from under him and catapulted him out into space. Deep into the back of the diving hornet the black spider-plane bored—and then they were one; were fused together in smoke and flames as they plunged to earth—with the dread glass-vapor tanks exploding in mid-air!

The hot breath of the blaze licked out for Wentworth as it

shot past him, but his black parachute opened above him and a gust of air carried him clear of that danger. Looking more than ever like a great black spider, he hovered over the deserted quadrangle and then dropped down into it as people came swarming from the doorways to close in around the fallen plane that had so recently threatened them with doom.

With stunning force Wentworth hit the ground and then was enveloped in the black folds of his 'chute. But he could not remain there, lying on the grass. He must not be caught and detained for questioning—with his task less than half-finished! His unyielding will prodded him to his knees as he unbuckled the parachute straps and wriggled out of them, set him to scurrying from beneath the black tent that covered him.

Through the milling throngs he worked his way to the Monroe Street entrance, where a score of mangled, bullet-torn bodies attested to the deadly fire that had frustrated every attempt at escape. That fire had come from the barroom across the way—the barroom from which Lefty Lomack had battered out the windows so that he and his thugs might have free range for their deadly typewriters hidden behind the protection of the bar.

Wentworth's fingers closed on one of the grenades he had taken from the cockpit of the Seversky, triggered the pin—and the deadly pear arced across the street. True to its mark! With a terrific crash, the entire front of that barroom was blasted to wreckage—and treacherous Lefty Lomack followed Patsy DeLott into eternity.

CHAPTER 13
BEYOND THE PANEL

EVEN BEFORE Wentworth reached Chinatown he knew about what to expect. The street in which Chen Ah-lo's bazaar was located was jammed with fire apparatus, and the building gushed smoke and flame from every window. Despite the efforts of the firemen, it was obvious that nothing but the outer shell of the structure would remain when that conflagration had burned itself out.

Chen Ah-lo had gone, taking no chances that his escaped prisoner might return with the police.

But there was another way to pick up his murderous trail, and Wentworth lost no time following it. Quickly he hailed a cab, and twenty minutes later the taxi drove him to the front of the East Thirty-sixth Street home of Austin Warrington—and of Wong, the valet.

Finger ready on his automatic trigger, Wentworth rang the bell and stood back from the door. But there was no response from within. Nothing—until he suddenly detected what seemed to be the noise of a violent struggle going on inside the building. Wentworth listened, and then the crash of furniture being overturned was unmistakable. Wentworth dashed the barrel of his weapon through the glass door and climbed through the shattered pane.

Now there was no doubt of the battle that raged at the rear of the floor. In Warrington's study, he guessed, as he ran down the hallway and crouched in the entrance. The place was a wreck, everything turned topsy-turvy. At first glance, he saw that the trail of Wong had reached its end. A few feet from the doorway the Chinaman's body lay sprawled, his head a ghastly mess where it had been bludgeoned with skull-shattering force.

Wong was dead, but Warrington was still alive. In the midst of the overturned furniture he was struggling frantically for his life. Flat on his back on the floor, he fought feebly against the grip of strong fingers that were choking the life out of him.

Wentworth sprang across the room—and stared down in amazement at that deadly struggle. The fellow astride Warrington was Dopey Weasel!

Snarling and drooling with rage, Dopey leaped to his feet and turned on this new antagonist. But Wentworth met his berserk rush with a pile-driving right that slammed him back on his heels. Before the furious gangster could charge again, Wentworth followed him up, drove him backward with a barrage of blows that sent him reeling against the wall.

For an instant he seemed to hang there, tottering—and then a gurgling scream burbled thickly from his throat as a footlong knife streaked across the room and sank almost hilt-deep in his throat!

Wentworth's perfect reflexes were all that saved his own life at that moment. Instinctively he ducked, threw himself hard to one side—just as a second knife whizzed past his ear and buried its sharp point deep in the wall panel against which Dopey Weasel had been standing. That deadly knife, quivering like a live thing in the wood, had been intended for the back of Wentworth's neck....

On his feet again in a instant, Wentworth whirled—but there was no sign of an attacker. Now the disordered study was empty except for himself and the Weasel—and the still body of Wong. Austin Warrington had disappeared, but it was impossible that the old man could have thrown those knives with such deadly accuracy and strength.

The Weasel was mortally wounded. "Wasn't your fault, Blinky," he gasped. "They'd've gotten me anyway. But I *did* want to get him… before I checked out. He's not her father, Blinky— not Sue's father. She's mine… Sue Warrington is my kid—my daughter, you hear that? I lost her years ago when she was a baby. You know why—the dope. I went away on a spree and when I come back her mother was gone… and took her along."

He shuddered. "I couldn't find any trace of them for years… and then I found out what had happened. Her mother was dead… and Austin Warrington had the kid… because his wife didn't have any of her own. I kept track of her after that, Blinky. I watched her grow up… but I had sense enough to keep away from her. I watched her… until the mummy death took her. Since then I been doing my damnedest to get the skunks that killed her. But… she… ain't dead, Blinky—she's *alive.*

"She ain't dead!" he wheezed again. "I don't want him to have her, Blinky! Promise me you won't let him! Promise me you'll get the dirty, murdering rat…."

Wentworth caught him as he slumped backward, lowered him gently to the floor, and saw that the gushing blood torrent had slowed. Dopey Weasel was dead, and as Wentworth looked down at the blood-smeared face he wondered if the man had not been mad.

Sue Warrington his daughter? That was possible—was in line with the half-suspicion that had been growing in Wentworth's mind. But that the girl was still alive—that was preposterous. Wentworth had seen her die, had beheld the horrible thing that was her mummified corpse....

RISING FROM beside the Weasel's slumped body, he stepped up to the knife that had almost taken his own life. He examined it closely. A blade of eight or nine inches with a carved ivory handle, it was a beautiful piece of work—an exquisite specimen of Chinese art that might have found a place in any connoisseur's collection. The force with which it had been thrown had driven it nearly halfway through the panel. But it moved from side to side freely when Wentworth grasped it.

That meant that the panel was thin—that there was no wall behind it. Wentworth moved closer and tested it with his knuckles. It rang hollowly. He pushed against it, and it gave slightly under the pressure.

Stepping back, he launched his foot against it—and the flimsy panel splintered. Half a dozen solid kicks reduced it to splinters and revealed a black opening behind it—that proved to be another room when he turned his flashlight into it.

Wriggling through the shattered panel, he located a light switch and snapped it on. He found himself in a small office with another room beyond it. This second room proved to be a small but completely equipped laboratory that had evidently been in use very recently. Its shelves were lined with bottles and a number of them were arranged on a center table on which some sort of distillation was still at work, the dark brown precipitate gathering in a round glass receptacle.

Wentworth sniffed the stuff and recoiled from the stench. It was like putrefying flesh and yet not quite that—an odor he could not identify. Puzzling over it, he went back into the other room—a combination office and small library, the shelves lined with well-thumbed books.

Austin Warrington had spent quite a number of years in Tibet and China. It was for that reason that Wentworth had wanted to talk to him, had wanted to probe his exact relationship with Wong—and perhaps with Chen Ah-lo. But he had had no idea that the retired explorer was as conversant as this with things Oriental, or that Warrington made a hobby of Chinese medicine....

Medical books were about all that the shelves of that cubby-hole library contained. The rest of the wall space was covered with framed photographs—and every one of them was of Sue Warrington, mostly taken during the last ten years of her life.

Thoughtfully he turned to the roll-top desk and searched it carefully. The pigeonholes yielded nothing of interest. But when he opened a deep lower drawer he almost gasped in surprise. That drawer was about a foot deep—and it was nearly filled with closely stacked bills of large denominations! Hundred-dollar bills! Thousand-dollar bills! That hoard must run up into the millions!

The packet he lifted from the drawer and rifled between his fingers totaled at least fifty thousand dollars—and there were hundreds more like it! Marveling, he ran his hand down into the drawer—and suddenly something pounced upon his back. A coat-sleeve whipped over his face from behind, knocked off his glasses and blindfolded him. Quickly he was yanked backward in the desk chair, and a cold gun muzzle ground into the side of his neck.

Wentworth did not try to struggle. "All right," a hard voice grated in his ear. "Take it very easy if you want to keep your skin whole. I'm going to release you, but if you try to pull anything—"

Abruptly the words stopped, and his captor whistled softly.

"Wentworth!" he jubilated. "This is better than I expected! Just like having ten thousand berries dropped in my lap!"

Warily Ted O'Neill, the *Chronicle* reporter, backed away, keeping his weapon trained carefully on Wentworth's heart.

"I sure didn't recognize you," he admitted, "but I had a hunch you'd show up here sooner or later. Thought this was a good place to go reward-hunting. When I saw you smash hell out of Warrington's front door I thought I'd better come in and have a look—and here you are, Richard Wentworth in the flesh!"

"So now all you have to do is call the cops and collect your blood money," Wentworth eyed him bitterly.

"Right you are, brother," the reporter grinned. "That's what I'm going to do right now, Mr. Wentworth, or the Spider, or whatever you call yourself in that outfit. You're stepping out through that broken panel with this gun kissing your spine—"

Like an eerie grave call, a shrill scream suddenly knifed through the stillness that lay between them—a muffled scream that seemed to come from a great distance. O'Neill's voice faltered and stopped. His eyes widened and flashed questioningly to Wentworth's. The pleased grin froze on his face, and he listened intently. There it was again—the thin ghost of a woman's scream that seemed to come from the laboratory, and with it the reporter's assurance vanished.

"That may be some trick of yours, Wentworth..." He hesitated—and in that moment Wentworth was upon him, knocking the gun in the air and smashing his fist home to the young fellow's jaw.

O'Neill staggered back and blinked groggily, and then the knockout blow caught him on the point of the chin and dropped him in a heap. Without so much as another glance at him, Wentworth whirled and dived into the laboratory. That scream he would have recognized anywhere on earth—it had been torn from the frightened lips of Nita van Sloan!

CHAPTER 14
HELL'S BATH

BAFFLED, WENTWORTH stood in the center of that laboratory. It was empty, of course, and there seemed to be only one door leading into it—the one through which he had come. Yet he was certain that Nita's scream had come from this direction.

He was just about to dash back through the office into Warrington's study when that distant scream knifed at him again. This time he definitely located it—knew that it had come from a closet at the end of the room. That closet was filled with medical supplies, but he flung his weight against the shelves—and the whole interior moved back half a dozen feet, to reveal a flight of steps leading down into the darkness.

Unhesitatingly Wentworth stepped into the opening and speared the darkness with his flash.

But for those screams he would have thought that he was alone there beneath the city, roaming through tunnels that had long been forgotten. Suddenly he tensed and held his light still. The corridor through which he was walking was somewhat wider than the others he had been in—but the end of it seemed narrower than it had been. It was!

The colorless gray wall ahead of him was closing in, narrowing the corridor until in a few moments it would become a dead end.

Instantly Wentworth leaped forward and sprinted across the intervening distance. Just in time he slipped through the narrowing opening—to find himself in what appeared to be a windowless, doorless room. With a dull thud the entrance through which he had come closed and was lost in the monotony of the unbroken walls.

A trap—and he had walked right into it!

But now the screams and moans were much closer. They seemed to come from right beside him—from *beneath* him. Carefully, he played the narrow beam of his light on the walls and ceiling, on the stone floor—and there he found what he wanted. In the center of the room was a trapdoor that fitted so closely that he could barely pry it loose.

BENEATH THAT trapdoor was a big circular room more than fifty feet in diameter—a deep cavern of a place that seemed to be hewn out of the solid rock. The bottom of the cavern was filled from side to side with a reddish liquid that was flowing into it from several points—a hellish crimson flood that looked like blood in the dim light of torches that played upon its surface and revealed the horror it engulfed.

In that crimson bath were half a dozen writhing victims who filled the cavern with their piteous screams as they fought vainly to keep their heads above the poison that already had doomed them. Men and women they had been when they had been cast into that hellish pool—but already their bodies were becoming emaciated, turning into gaunt mummies!

Frantic to escape the doom that had fastened upon them, they splashed and floundered toward a ledge which ran along one side of the cavern, some twenty feet below the roof and a little more than a foot above the liquid surface—but that ledge was manned by hell's own spawn. Four weird-looking creatures, who were naked to the waist and had the heads and torsos of ghastly mummies—they took fiendish pleasure in their diabolical task.

Whenever one of the pleading victims came within reach of even the futile sanctuary that ledge would afford, one of the leering devils acted. He leaned over with a sharp-pointed trident and stabbed pitilessly at the clutching fingers, lashed at the bobbing heads with metal-tipped whips and forced them back beneath the crimson surface.

Wentworth felt cold sweat oozing out all over him as he stared down helplessly at this awful suffering. Then all strength seemed to seep out of him, to leave him crouching limply at the edge of the trap. In that moment he had switched his position so that he could see the other side of the cavern—and what he beheld completely enervated him.

On that side of the great room was another ledge, higher above the poisonous bath than the other. Here four more of those appalling—looking mummy creatures presided—and sitting helpless at their feet were more than a dozen securely bound victims. Wentworth stared, and his eyes fastened on the grim countenance of Jackson, on the utterly dejected figure of Kenneth Rockwell—and on the pitifully brave face of Nita van Sloan!

Now a scream that was the epitome of all human terror rang through the cavern and two of those bestial mummies lifted a girl to her feet and dragged her to the edge of the ledge. Holding her helpless there, they cut the ropes which bound her arms and legs—then flung her wide, to pitch head-first into the crimson death-bath!

Wentworth's blood ran cold as that soul-penetrating scream knifed into his ears and then was abruptly stilled by the sound of the luckless victim's splash. For a brief moment horrified silence gripped the cavern; even the half-mad sufferers in the pool stilled their moans—and into the silence boomed a deep voice that seemed to come from nowhere.

"Another whose husband was so stupid as to think he could defy the commands of the Withering Death!" it taunted. "How unfortunate that he cannot be here to watch her take her bath— unless, perhaps, you up there at the trap *are* her husband. You wanted to see what was going on down here, and now you shall see, my friend. You shall have a box seat, until it is your turn in the pool."

Wentworth drew back from the trapdoor the moment that mocking voice began. Swiftly his agile fingers went to work on his face, while his eyes never left that hell below him. What he saw there tightened an icy grip around his heart, made him hurry his transformation as he had never hurried before. Two of those heartless beasts were bending again, now taking hold of Nita and dragging her to the edge of the ledge.

"And now we have a foolish girl who thought she could interfere with the will of the Withering Death—after her meddlesome fiancé had already doomed her by intruding himself in other people's affairs." The booming voice dripped with unctuous mock-reproach. "Unfortunately, the police make it inconvenient for Mr. Wentworth to be here to join her."

Out from beneath his vest Wentworth took a long, thin but remarkably strong silken rope, unwound it swiftly and then fastened one end of it securely around a hinge of the trapdoor. The other end he tied to his belt. Quickly the black wig and hat went into place, the black cape was flung over his shoulder, and he dropped to the floor.

Nita's bonds had been cut. At the very edge of the ledge she tried to push back, tried to grab those hideous mummy creatures and cling to them—but they laughed at her struggles. Prying her fingers loose, they whipped her arms behind her back—and flung her out into space!

That was the moment the Spider dived through the trap. One arm clutching the silken cord to break his fall, he plummeted like the insect whose name he had adopted. Like a pendulum he swung with the impetus of his leap—and just as Nita hit the crimson bath, as her feet splashed into it, his arms whipped around her waist and snatched her to safety.

INSTANTLY HE had her securely under his arm, and her hold tightened on him. Freeing one hand, he blasted sudden death into those callous devils on the upper ledge. Two of them dropped beneath his fire. Then the arc of his swing carried him within reach of the ledge, his feet touched it—and he was in their midst, grabbing at them, lashing out at them with the pistol barrel, smashing it down at the horrible masks they wore over their faces.

Seconds of bitter, merciless fighting—and then the ledge was cleared of the mummy masqueraders. Now the prisoners could be released. Dropping down beside Jackson, Wentworth tore at the ropes that held him, while Nita started to release Kenneth Rockwell. But the danger was not yet past. The round walls of that cavern room were studded with porthole-like openings near the ceiling, and from one of them a pistol opened fire.

Springing in front of Nita to shield her with his body, Wentworth's guns blasted a quick reply that drove the marksman from his position. But out of the porthole came that familiar mocking voice.

"Stay there then, if that is what you prefer, Mr. Spider," it taunted. "You and your little party can remain there for the rest of time—unless, of course, you become thirsty and want to take a little dip in the pond below you. On second thought, that is much better than wasting lead on you. Farewell, my friend.

Perhaps I shall meet you in eternity—and you will know enough to keep out of my affairs!"

The mocking devil behind that porthole was escaping, abandoning them there, but the Spider was not yet finished. Leaping from the ledge, he swung out into space and started climbing, hand over hand, up the silken rope to the trapdoor. Halfway to the top he paused and glanced up at the black opening above him—and stared into the grinning face of Chen Ah-lo!

Chen Ah-lo leaning out of the trapdoor with a keen-bladed knife that pressed against the silken rope!

"You work hard," he chuckled evilly, "and for what purpose? You will go down much more quickly than you come up. The moment I cut through this thin rope—"

Below Wentworth the deadly poison bath waited. Above him the implacable Chinese blocked his only escape. There was no way out, no hope. One swipe of that blade and his fate was sealed.

But at that moment the round face of the Chinese became almost comical as his eyes bulged and his mouth gaped open. Just for a second, and then it was yanked back from the trapdoor as the knife shot past Wentworth's head and plopped harmlessly into the crimson pool.

Hand over hand—and then the Spider pulled himself over the edge of the trap opening and switched on his flashlight, to play its beam around the upper room until it centered on two men locked in a writhing, struggling heap on the floor. A Chinese and a white man, but just as the light picked them out the white man got the upper hand. Tearing his gun-wrist free from the other's grip, he pounded the weapon down on the Oriental's head—and a shot roared thunderously in the low room.

That shot blew away half of Chen Ah-lo's skull....

"He had it coming to him, the bloody murderer!" Ted O'Neill panted as he scrambled to his feet, still holding the bloodied gun. "Let's make a truce, Spider," he offered suddenly. "I found out tonight that I've been wrong about you. That murdering Chink is the answer to all these mummy deaths. He murdered Warrington here tonight. I just saw the poor devil's emaciated body—"

O'Neill led the way on the run, out through the opening which had again materialized at the side of the room, down a corridor and into a bare cell of a room. There, chained to an iron bed, lay a gaunt skeleton of a creature in the clothing Austin Warrington had been wearing only a short while before—a mummy that any of his associates would have identified as the remains of the retired scientist.

But Wentworth took no more than a glance at the poor wretch. Then he was out of the cell again, combing that maze of corridors and empty cubbyholes until he found a door that would not open.

"Use all your strength against it—we've got to get in there," he barked to O'Neill, and then led the way with a crashing charge that rattled the door in its frame.

Into a room that was almost as bare as the chained mummy's cell they plunged—a room with a bed against one wall and a single chair against two others. In front of that bed, trying to hide the face of the girl who lay stretched out on it, stood the threatening figure of Chen Ah-lo.

"The Chink!" Ted O'Neill gasped in bewilderment. "But I just killed him—he's back there with a hole blown in his skull—"

Then he caught a glimpse of the girl who was sitting on the bed, blinking her eyes as if awakening from a deep sleep.

"Holy hell!" he half-whispered. "That's Sue Warrington—and she's *alive!* The Chink—and now her! Either I'm nuts—or this damn place must be a corner of eternity!"

WENTWORTH HAD recognized the girl, also—and with that recognition much of the fog that had cloaked his brain for so long began to lift. One by one his half-formed suspicions began to jibe, the pieces to fall into place—and the rage that seethed in his soul knew no bounds. Grimly his steely eyes shifted from the dazed girl to the figure in front of her—just as one of those capacious sleeves moved ever so slightly.

That was all—just a bellying of a sleeve and an almost imperceptible widening of those slant eyes. But that was sufficient. Wentworth's leap came almost simultaneously with the spurt of flame that blazed through the silken shield—almost but not quite. A split-second faster he had got under way. The bullet tore through the black cape and seared his ribs like a red-hot iron, but before the trigger could be pressed a second time the Spider's black arms were wrapped around his victim.

Desperately, the yellow man tried to bring his weapon to bear on his attacker, tugged and twisted mightily—until it seemed that his arm would be snapped off at the shoulder. Helplessly, his pain-wracked fingers opened and released their grip, but the moment the gun thudded to the bed behind him the last vestige of sanity deserted him. Stark fear flared in his eyes and turned him into a wild man—into a creature who fought with the savagery of a jungle beast.

Clawing, kicking, scratching, viciously trying to bite, he flung himself at that relentless black figure—only to be smashed back time and again by coolly directed blows, to be seized in sinewy arms and hurled aside, to be grabbed and throttled as his clawing hands flailed the air. Deliberately Wentworth pounded away at that round, fat face, ripping and tearing at it with his punishing fists, twisting and distorting it, hammering the very flesh from the bones—

But that yellowish substance that came off on his hands was not flesh. It was make-up material, grease-paint, putty, artificial flesh. It peeled off in chunks and scabs as his fingers tore at the snarling face—stripped off and uncovered the hardly recognizable features of a white man beneath the yellow mask.

"Warrington!" came in an incredulous exclamation from young Ted O'Neill, who hovered on the edge of that battle.

That damning recognition drove the old man into utter frenzy. Screaming like an idiot, he hurled Wentworth aside with inhuman strength and leaped onto one of the room's two chairs, his right hand clutching for what seemed to be a ventilator chain that hung beside it.

Even before he had grabbed the chain, Wentworth had divined his purpose and was up from the floor, to leap onto the chair beside him.

"Grab hold of a piece of furniture and hang on!" he shouted a warning to O'Neill—just as the floor of the room gave way.

As if it were on hinges, that whole floor sagged at one end and dropped down, to leave the furniture, which was fastened to the walls, suspended in space! Suspended above that deadly poison bath cavern!

That much Wentworth glimpsed as the floor vanished, and then he had his hands full with the frenzied madman who shared his precarious perch. Desperately they struggled, locked in each other's arms, teetering dizzily on the edge of the seat. That battle could have only one result. There was barely room on the chair for their feet had they stood still, but locked in this mad struggle….

Wentworth's fingers fastened in the madman's throat, forced his head backward against the wall—but that gave Warrington the purchase he needed. Putting all his strength in his shoulders, he heaved his body forward, and they toppled off into space, pitching down to the doom that awaited them twenty feet below.

Twenty feet—a fraction of a second! But in that infinitesimal flash of eternity Wentworth's fist whipped up with all his strength and his knees jackknifed into Warrington's midriff. Hurling the madman away from him, he twisted his body through the air, threw himself to one side so that he grazed the side wall. Frantically he clutched for a handhold, and his fingers fastened on the now deserted upper ledge just as Warrington, half-swathed in the billowing folds of the Spiders black cape which he had torn loose, splashed into the pool of death!

PERCHED ON the bed outside Sue Warrington, Ted

O'Neill stared down and watched death write finis to that grim struggle—and then turned to consider his own unenviable position. How he was going to get across that floorless room to the chain which would restore it to normal, he had no idea. Nor had he solved the problem when the door of the room opened and Kenneth Rockwell teetered on the brink of the threshold, with Nita, Jackson and the other rescued victims behind him.

Leaping from the doorway to the chair beside the floor chain was a desperate hazard, but Rockwell made it, and in a few moments he was clasping Sue Warrington in his arms. Still under the effects of a stupefying drug, she could only cling to him and sob, could only walk at his side as he followed the others through that interminable maze of corridors.

They were still trying to find a way out of that maze when Richard Wentworth arrived at the door of Austin Warrington's home with Commissioner Kirkpatrick and a squad of police. In the bewildering labyrinth the rescuers found them—to Ted O'Neill's wide-eyed amazement. Impetuously he started to speak, and then held his tongue, as Wentworth led the way up, not into the Warrington house but into the boarded-up mansion on Park Avenue that had been Nita's undoing.

"You remember this place, Kirk," he was telling the police commissioner. "It was built fifty years ago by Eli Stackpool. He always had a yen for trick doors and passages, and when he retired with more money than he could ever spend, he indulged his hobby here. The place is a regular madhouse, but it has been closed up for years. Somehow Austin Warrington must have learned of it and bought it and then connected it by underground passages with his own house on the side street behind it."

Stanley Kirkpatrick nodded understanding, but his eyes were full of questions, his brow lined with wrinkles.

"Even such a crazy maze is simple compared to the complexities of this wild case," he complained. "Warrington must have been crazy—"

"He was—undoubtedly," Wentworth nodded. "He had spent too much time in the Orient, away from white women, after the death of his wife—and when he came home he fell in love with his adopted daughter. An unhealthy love that coveted her secretly and schemed to keep her for himself by driving away all her suitors. That worked until Rockwell came along, but then Warrington saw that he was licked—and he went crazy altogether."

"He put me through hell," Rockwell said bitterly. "First he made me believe that Sue was dead. God knows that was bad enough. But it was infinitely worse to discover that she was still alive, a prisoner faced with that horrible death I had already seen so much of. With that threat hanging over me I was helpless; I had to obey whatever orders came to me over the telephone. That is why I led you into that trap at the Sedgwick sanitarium, Wentworth. But I didn't know you were to be killed there. I thought they merely intended to incarcerate you there to keep you out of their way. When I saw the explosion it was too late—I was grabbed and thrown into a car and brought to this place."

"But, even so, I don't see how Warrington thought all this would get him anywhere with the girl," Kirkpatrick puzzled.

"She still would have thought she was his daughter—still would have been in love with Rockwell."

"That is what any normal man would conclude," Wentworth agreed, "but Warrington was not normal—he was crazy. In his desperation, when he saw that he could not dispose of Rockwell as easily as the others, he devised a scheme that would give him what he wanted and at the same time feed his bitter hatred. He knew Chen Ah-lo from his days in China and had kept in touch with the man in this country. Between them they devised the ghastly extortion scheme that has terrorized New York—based on a poisonous drug that Warrington discovered in the course of his experiments in search of a chemical compound that would give him everlasting youth."

"Everlasting youth!" Kirkpatrick was incredulous.

"He thought he had found it," Rockwell corroborated soberly. "While I was a prisoner here he came down and gloated over me. He told me about the stuff—told me how it would make him young again, would change his whole appearance so that he could woo Sue and make her love him. With limitless wealth he intended to take her abroad, to start a new life—"

"The Austin Warrington the world knew was to die," Wentworth pieced the mad pattern together. "That is the reason for that poor devil of a mummy chained in that cell downstairs. He was to be the Austin Warrington the police would find when they raided this place and discovered young Rockwell supposedly bossing it. You know how much evidence you already have against Rockwell, Kirk—faked evidence, every bit of it. Deliberately planted so that Rockwell would go to the chair for these mummy murders. With Rockwell electrocuted, Warrington's insane jealousy would have been satisfied and his competition for Sue's affection would have been eliminated."

"But Chen Ah-lo—where did he figure in the money end?" Kirkpatrick wondered.

"Chen Ah-lo was as unscrupulous as Warrington," Wentworth answered thoughtfully. "He betrayed his own people shamelessly, undoubtedly intending to split the money with Warrington, in whose hidden room it was stored."

"An utterly insane scheme," Stanley Kirkpatrick said slowly. "Almost incredible in its madness—but all criminals are mad. It is only a question of how far their madness carries them."

"Amen to that," Ted O'Neill agreed fervently. "Matter of fact, I am beginning to feel slightly cuckoo myself, Commissioner. Here I kill a man—and then see him standing up there and fighting another man! Again, the Spider was dead—shriveled to a mummy in his own house, the papers said—and here he was alive, fighting in this madhouse! But one thing is sure," he finished grimly, "he's dead now. I saw him splash into that hellish pool."

"And it is also the end of these ridiculous charges against Richard Wentworth, Stanley," Nita reminded. "Perhaps now you will be willing to withdraw your reward offer—"

The end of the Spider… Stanley Kirkpatrick's saturnine face was enigmatic as he met her eyes, but he nodded slowly.

"One of his last acts was to deliver a container, filled with that mummy poison, to the General Hospital," he said quietly. "That was what the doctors needed. This morning I heard that they have discovered the antidote and are using it to treat the victims. That is the way I would have wanted the Spider to end—"

But his eyes were quizzical as he watched Richard Wentworth hand Nita into a taxicab and watched them drive off together. The Spider finished? Whether he was or not—Stanley Kirkpatrick knew that that grim figure of dark justice had once more taken the final trick and the game.

POPULAR HERO PULPS AVAILABLE NOW:

ACE G-MAN

❑ #1: The Suicide Squad Reports for Death	$14.95
❑ #2: Coffins for the Suicide Squad	$14.95
❑ #3: Shells for the Suicide Squad	$14.95

OPERATOR 5

❑ #1: The Masked Invasion	$13.95
❑ #2: The Invisible Empire	$13.95
❑ #3: The Yellow Scourge	$13.95
❑ #4: The Melting Death	$13.95
❑ #5: Cavern of the Damned	$13.95
❑ #6: Master of Broken Men	$13.95
❑ #7: Invasion of the Dark Legions	$13.95
❑ #8: The Green Death Mists	$13.95
❑ #9: Legions of Starvation	$13.95
❑ #10: The Red Invader	$13.95
❑ #11: The League of War-Monsters	$13.95
❑ #12: The Army of the Dead	$13.95
❑ #13: March of the Flame Marauders	$13.95
❑ #14: Blood Reign of the Dictator	$13.95
❑ #15: Invasion of the Yellow Warlords	$13.95
❑ #16: Legions of the Death Master	$13.95
❑ #17: Hosts of the Flaming Death	$13.95
❑ #18: Invasion of the Crimson Death Cult	$13.95
❑ #19: Attack of the Blizzard Men	$13.95
❑ #20: Scourge of the Invisible Death	$13.95
❑ #21: Raiders of the Red Death	$13.95
❑ #22: War-Dogs of the Green Destroyer	$13.95
❑ #23: Rockets From Hell	$13.95
❑ #24: War-Masters from the Orient	$13.95
❑ #25: Crime's Reign of Terror	$13.95
❑ #26: Death's Ragged Army	$13.95
❑ #27: Patriots' Death Battalion	$13.95
❑ #28: The Bloody Forty-five Days	$13.95
❑ #29: America's Plague Battalions	$13.95
❑ #30: Liberty's Suicide Legions	$13.95
❑ #31: Siege of the Thousand Patriots	$13.95
❑ #32: Patriots' Death March	$14.95
❑ #33: Revolt of the Lost Legions	$14.95
❑ #34: Drums of Destruction	$14.95
❑ **NEW:** #35: The Army Without a Country	$14.95

CAPTAIN COMBAT

❑ #1: The Sky Beast of Berlin	$13.95
❑ #2: Red Wings For the Blood Battalion	$13.95
❑ #3: Low Ceiling For Nazi Hell Hawks	$13.95

DUSTY AYRES AND HIS BATTLE BIRDS

❑ #1: Black Lightning!	$13.95
❑ #2: Crimson Doom	$13.95
❑ #3: The Purple Tornado	$13.95
❑ #4: The Screaming Eye	$13.95
❑ #5: The Green Thunderbolt	$13.95
❑ #6: The Red Destroyer	$13.95
❑ #7: The White Death	$13.95
❑ #8: The Black Avenger	$13.95
❑ #9: The Silver Typhoon	$13.95
❑ #10: The Troposphere F-S	$13.95
❑ #11: The Blue Cyclone	$13.95
❑ #12: The Tesla Raiders	$13.95

MAVERICKS

❑ #1: Five Against the Law	$12.95
❑ #2: Mesquite Manhunters	$12.95
❑ #3: Bait for the Lobo Pack	$12.95
❑ #4: Doc Grimson's Outlaw Posse	$12.95
❑ #5: Charlie Parr's Gunsmoke Cure	$12.95

THE MYSTERIOUS WU FANG

❑ #1: The Case of the Six Coffins	$12.95
❑ #2: The Case of the Scarlet Feather	$12.95
❑ #3: The Case of the Yellow Mask	$12.95
❑ #4: The Case of the Suicide Tomb	$12.95
❑ #5: The Case of the Green Death	$12.95
❑ #6: The Case of the Black Lotus	$12.95
❑ #7: The Case of the Hidden Scourge	$12.95

THE SECRET 6

❑ #1: The Red Shadow	$13.95
❑ #2: House of Walking Corpses	$13.95
❑ #3: The Monster Murders	$13.95
❑ #4: The Golden Alligator	$13.95

CAPTAIN ZERO

❑ #1: City of Deadly Sleep	$13.95
❑ #2: The Mark of Zero!	$13.95
❑ #3: The Golden Murder Syndicate	$13.95